Child of Time

The Pearl Watch

Allie Marie

CHILD OF TIME

CHILD OF TIME

The Pearl Watch

Book 5 of the True Colors Series

Copyright ©2019 by Allie Marie

Published by Nazzaro & Price Publishing

Published in the United States of America

Allie Marie

BOOKS BY ALLIE MARIE

THE TRUE COLORS SERIES

Teardrops of the Innocent: The White Diamond Story (Book 1)

Heart of Courage: The Red Ruby Story (Book 2)

Voice of the Just: The Blue Sapphire (Book 3)

Hands of the Healer: The Christmas Emerald (Book 4)

ANTHOLOGIES

"'TIS THE SEASON"

It's a Wonderful Life After All

(Sweet Romance Novelettes with D. F. Jones and others)

DEDICATION

For Bernetta
RIP, sweet friend

ACKNOWLEDGMENTS

When I put the final touches on the last book of <u>The True Colors Series</u>, a moment of sadness swept over me as I said farewell to my modern characters and their 18th century counterparts. As I wrote each new book, there were many surprise twists and turns that I hadn't seen coming, but I have thoroughly enjoyed the challenge of twisting and turning with each written word.

While this series ends with *Child of Time: The Pearl Watch*, I suspect the characters will make cameo appearances in <u>The True Spirits Trilogy</u> planned for next year. It will be like seeing old friends again.

I owe a world of gratitude to the many people who make it possible for me to fulfill my writing dreams and bring this series to fruition.

To my husband Jack, and to our sons and families, for unwavering love and support.

To Sandi and Laura for patience and diligence in reading my drafts—and then reading the many revisions. Thank you, Dawn, Kathleen, and Penny, for the extra eyes on the final version.

To my editor Helen Brown Nazzaro and publisher/cover artist James Price for the continuing support, friendship, and assistance you always provide as we finished each book in the True Colors Series.

To Laura Somers Photography, for your contributions that enabled James to create yet another perfect cover for *Child of Time: The Pearl Watch*.

I am grateful to all the readers who enjoy my stories,

especially the ladies at the Windsor Book Club.

I have to give a shout out to my "Team AllieKats." I can't thank you enough for your support and enthusiasm.

Many local businesses have provided support for me on this journey, especially The Bier Garden, Dennis' Spaghetti and Steakhouse, Jalapenos, Roger Brown's Restaurant and Sports Bar, and the Little Shoppes on High. I am truly grateful.

To Carrie Hankes, thank you for answering a new round of questions about the colonial times in Yorktown. I made several visits to the American Revolution Museum at Yorktown, Virginia, to capture the essence of the period through their many displays and exhibits, including the Continental Army Encampment. I also referred many times to their website for information. You can find out more about the Siege at Yorktown at: https://www.historyisfun.org/.

Online resources used:

https://ahec.armywarcollege.edu/trail/Redoubt10/index.cfm

Allie Marie

CONTENTS

PROLOGUE

Portsmouth, Virginia
1861

My name is Maggie and I am eight. I know I shouldn't have taken the velvet bag with Mama's watch and Papa's ring, but I couldn't help myself. I love to look at the shiny jewelry

The other children are so mean to me. I won't come out when they yell my name, even though I can hear them running around, looking for me. But they won't find me hidden in the magnolia tree. They are afraid to crawl under the leaves and come into the cave the branches make. They think it is haunted.

But I'm not afraid of ghosts, even though the other kids call me a baby. I like to sit in the tree and let the wind blow the leaves.

I open the cover of Mama's pretty pearl watch. The big hand points almost to the twelve and the little hand points to three. Papa taught me how to tell time. It will be three o'clock very soon.

Thunder crashes over my head, and I drop the jewelry. The winds whip my hair across my face, and it stings. I scramble down the tree trunk but I miss the bottom limb and fall on my back, knocking the breath out of me.

The storm is punishing me for taking the pouch. I get up but can't find my way from under the tree. I push through the branches as another clap of thunder brings raindrops so sharp, they feel like needles on my skin. Piercing twigs tear at my clothes and try to snatch my doll Abby from my arms. I pull her free and stumble through the branches just as a wagon arrives.

Mama calls my name but when I try to answer her, the rain splashes into my mouth and chokes me. I try to scream for her to come for me, but hands lift me from my feet, and I am pulled into a spinning black tunnel.

CHAPTER 1

Richmond, VA Seven years earlier

Daniel Lawrence's rapid stride took him past the display window. Taking two steps backwards, he skidded to a stop in front of the glass. He peeked inside, his gaze settling on the item that had attracted his attention.

Specks of light sparkled off of a ladies' gold brooch watch, trimmed with a circle of miniature pearls rimming the heart-shaped glass face. The hands pointed toward twelve o'clock.

"That's it," he mumbled aloud. He stepped inside the shop.

Behind the counter, a man studied a diamond through a jeweler's loupe. He glanced up and nodded. "What can I help you with today, good sir?"

"That ladies' watch in the window, the brooch? I'd like to see that." Daniel pointed toward the window.

The jeweler pushed his eyeshade higher on his head and walked to the shelf. He removed the watch and handed it to Daniel, who said, "My wife just gave birth to a baby daughter, and I have been looking for something unique to give her."

"This brooch is a perfect gift for her." The jeweler beamed with the potential for a sale. "And should you wish to make this brooch into a necklace, there is a small loop through which you can add a

1

chain that would enable your wife to wear this as a pendant watch as well."

"Quite undoubtedly baby Margaret will find it a fascinating distraction when she is old enough to look around," Daniel remarked.

"Margaret, did you say?"

"Yes, named after my wife's mother."

"Well," the jeweler said as he pulled his shade onto his forehead. "You could not have chosen a more appropriate gift for your wife. Did you know that Margaret comes from the Greek word for pearl?"

"Is that so?" Daniel turned the watch over. The smooth surface would be perfect for an engraved message.

"What do you think, good sir?"

"It's perfect." Daniel studied the brooch again and nodded. He handed it to the shopkeeper. "I'll take it."

Modern day Portsmouth, Virginia

Kirby Lawrence sank onto the edge of the bed, staring at the phone. The new life he had envisioned embarking upon had just been derailed with the four words on the screen.

"Call me. I'm pregnant."

Liana's text message delivered a single punch to his gut, as harsh as a fisted hand. He pressed his fingers to his eyes. He couldn't even remember the last time he and Liana had made love before they broke up. Three months, maybe more? They'd been living on different schedules—and distant lives—for the better part of the last twelve months.

Kirby leaned forward, jabbing his elbows onto his knees. He framed his face with his hands, shaking his head from side to side.

Why now? Why a child now, after more than three years together? Work took them on separate paths more often than it brought them together. Their busy careers, his as a Navy physician and hers as a jewelry boutique owner, had been the deciding factor in not having children.

Liana's increasingly erratic behavior had widened the growing chasm.

Kirby suspected Liana suffered from bipolar disorder. Her mood swings, barely exhibited in their early relationship, had become more frequent. Bouts of inexplicable jealousy warred with her cloying affection.

They both knew it had been over between them for months, and if neither had accepted it, the night he caught Liana with her lover had sealed the deal. After their breakup, the constant bombardment of nasty emails had caused him to block her phone.

Until her bombshell text arrived under a new number.

Kirby reread the four words that would shatter the happiness he had just found with Sandi Cross. Their time together had been short, but he was already in love with the beautiful lawyer and adored her energetic daughter Norrie.

Little Norrie—a child lost in time. Lost in some kind of time warp while her nineteenth-century counterpart Margaret slept in a bed downstairs.

Every moment of the events that led to their journey crammed into his head.

When they last stood in the parlor of Clothiste's Inn, an unbelievable twist of fate had taken him, Sandi, and her daughter through a time portal in the antique mirror which sent them to the eighteenth century. They arrived on the cusp of the siege of Yorktown.

Kirby landed in the dangerous times of colonial America while Sandi and Norrie were swept into life in a

French Army encampment in Yorktown, where they met a young girl named Margaret.

A more disturbing twist of fate occurred when they were swept back to their own time and discovered that young Margaret had returned with them instead of Norrie.

Through the closed bedroom door, muffled voices signaled the arrival of the other couples. Three of the voices belonged to the women who had each descended from a daughter of a French Army captain and his Acadian wife. Kirby, a descendant of the lone son, and the women had planned the gathering to figure out a way to transcend time to rescue Norrie and finally return Maggie home.

Kirby flopped onto his back and stared at the ceiling. If the descendants of Étienne and Clothiste were unsuccessful, Maggie would remain in the twenty-first century and Norrie—who knew where?

Sandi's face flashed through his mind. The single mother had severed ties with the father and raised Norrie alone. Her daughter was her world.

How can I break Liana's news to her? He had to figure out what to say. Her attention focused on finding Norrie but he could not hide the facts from her for long.

Before he had the chance to dwell on the dilemma, a light rap sounded at his door. He raised his head, then closed his eyes and shook his head in slight turns. *Go away, Sandi. I can't face you right now.*

"Kirby?" The voice did not belong to Sandi.

He relaxed as Stephanie's voice greeted him through the oak barrier. Scrambling to his feet, he reached for the door.

"Hey, Steph." He smiled at the petite woman whose ancestry research had dug up old bones in her family tree.

Literally and figuratively speaking.

"Are you all right, Kirby? You look like—you know. You haven't seen a ghost, have you?"

"No, I just got up too fast." Kirby smiled at the reference to "ghost." Clothiste's Inn, the Bed and Breakfast in which they stood, had a history of ghostly haunting, but he had never encountered an ethereal being.

Unless going back in time and meeting your ancestors counted as a ghostly encounter.

"Everyone's arrived, Kirby. We have some food and can get started…" Stephanie's voice trailed off and she fought back tears. He imagined her troubled look mirrored the one on his face.

"We'll get Norrie back," he reassured her, patting her shoulder. She smiled and patted his hand before turning to go back downstairs.

He stepped forward to follow, then stopped long enough to tap the screen of his phone. He clicked on the mute icon and swiveled on one heel to toss the phone on the bed.

No good news could come from that device tonight.

He reached the landing. A sundry mix of smells wafted up the stairwell and he inhaled with appreciation. Garlic, tomato sauce, and basil aromas sent his taste buds into overdrive. Although his time travels had taken him physically out of the 21st century for less than one full day, he had lived through months and years in the 18th.

His stomach growled, reminding him it had technically been more than two and a half centuries since his last meal.

***

Liana Chambers dialed Kirby's number. When his

voicemail kicked in, she said, "Kirby, I don't know where you are or why you haven't called me back, but we need to talk about this baby business." She smashed her finger on the red phone icon to end the call. She considered it a good sign that Kirby had not blocked her new number.

That was, if he had even gotten her message. *That asshole better not be screening my calls.* She narrowed her eyes at her cell, then shrugged.

He would call her.

He might be pissed at her message, but Kirby Lawrence was far too honorable a man not to deal with the situation the right way.

Her way.

A catlike smile spread across her face, then her gaze fell on a huge brown box beside her dining table. She'd attended an estate sale in Richmond recently and had bought two oversized brass genie bottles worth five times what she paid for them. Nearly two feet tall, the matching pair had long narrow necks and oval-shaped bases. Upon seeing them, she'd thought them larger but somewhat uglier versions of the ornate bottle in the opening credits of the old "I Dream of Jeannie" television series. She was about to pass on purchasing them when she saw the ridiculously low price and decided to buy the set. A craftsman could repurpose the ornate twins into gorgeous table lamps.

She rubbed her hands together in glee, then reached for a cotton cloth. "Will my genie appear?" she asked aloud as she brushed the soft fabric in circular motions across the etched metal.

No brocade-clad figure vaporized before her as she rubbed her way around the base.

"Genie?" she called. "Jinni? Hello, Djinni? Anybody home?" With a laugh, she pulled out the stopper. About three inches in diameter, the brass top held a dried, darkened cork. Bits and pieces broke off and tumbled down the neck. Liana went to the kitchen for a couple of cotton dishtowels. Spreading them across the table, she emptied the crumbled cork onto the first towel and satisfied she had removed all of the contents from the bottle, she replaced the metal stopper.

She repeated the process with the second bottle. The brass top seemed wedged and she had to twist and tug. As she pulled the plug loose, the cork crumbled into hundreds of tiny pieces.

"Shit," she muttered under her breath. She flipped the bottle upside down and tapped. Cork particles formed a small mound as they tumbled from the opening. As she turned the urn upright, the tinkle of something metallic fell back down the neck, the pinging sound swirling along the thin tube shape. She tipped the bottle over and tapped lightly. A few more flakes of cork trailed from the long neck, and the pinging sound swirled along, but stopped. Liana gave one vigorous shake to empty the debris, smacking the bottom. A woman's ring fell into the crumble of cork.

Liana set the bottle to the side and examined the ring. Small in circumference, perhaps made for a diminutive woman, the gold band circled to a filigreed upper shank. A small diamond sparkled atop the setting, at least equal in price to what she paid for the bottles. Liana's loupe was in her purse, but she knew in an instant the diamond was of a high quality. She picked up the bottle and shook again. Another metal ping circled the bowl, muffled to silence when she stood the bottle upright. She flipped the end over, tapping the bottom. A pearl earring stud slipped out.

Liana peered down the cavity. Unable to see inside,

she tilted the bottleneck toward the chandelier, but the ray of light could not reach the bottom. She pushed up the sleeve of her sweater and ran her thin arm down the length.

Her fingertips touched soft cloth but she was unable to maneuver in the narrow channel to get a better grip. Criss-crossing her fingers in a scissor-like motion, Liana gripped the edge of the material and pulled. Five times the bulky material refused to budge, but on the sixth try she had enough cloth to gain hold. Within seconds, she was able to pull the cloth along the neck until she could see the dark blue velvet cloth at the rim. She tugged, and the material ripped free with a splitting sound. A few jewels spewed out as if shot from a volcano, but the brass container resounded with the pings and swishes of jewelry falling back to the bottom.

One last time, she turned the bottle over.

Now unencumbered by the velvet cloth, dozens of jewelry pieces emptied from the neck. The mate to the pearl stud rolled to across the table and landed on the floor.

Liana's mouth formed a perfect "O" as she stared at the mother lode of necklaces, rings, and other adornments piling onto the table.

"Well, double shit," she said, as she raked her hands through the pile of gold and silver metals dotted with stones of red, green, blue, and white.

She reached forward and used her right ring finger to separate a gold chain from the mix. Tethered to the chain was an antique woman's gold timepiece. A circle of tiny seed pearls was embedded around a heart-shaped glass face marred with scratches and a large crack. She flipped it to over and studied the back, concluding that the watch might have once been a brooch that someone had fashioned into a necklace. She ran her fingers over the surface. The gold seemed to hum in her fingertips.

Have I seen this before?

She peered closer. In her line of business, she handled dozens of pieces every day, and preferred sleek modern adornments over the heavy ornate designs often found in antique jewelry.

She frowned, shrugged, and set it aside.

In the hands of the right jeweler, the old-fashioned piece could be restored to its former beauty and value. She knew just the person who could do it.

She calculated its potential restored value as she reached for a tissue to wrap the timepiece.

In a split second, Kirby Lawrence and pregnancy problems vanished far from her mind.

***

Kirby did not enter the dining room right away but instead observed the activity in progress from the shadows of the parlor. Sandi's law partner Terry Dunbar placed wine glasses on the right of glasses already filled with ice water, while Stephanie positioned napkins and silverware at each setting. Ginger-haired Mary Jo Cooper, the former soldier who now owned a French café, arranged pastries on platters.

His distant cousins. Three women with whom he shared a common set of seventh great-grandparents with ties to the American Revolution.

Étienne and Clothiste de la Rocher—ancestors he'd just met, thanks to a freaky incident that sent him back in time to their colonial lives and then spit him back to the 21st century.

He'd learned bits and pieces of the history that

brought the family from France and Canada to America.

Kirby stirred from his reverie as Gage Dunbar entered the dining room, carrying two uncorked bottles of wine to the table. The firefighter stopped to plant a kiss on his fiancée Stephanie's nose before setting the bottles to the side. This task completed, he passed her again and swept her into his arms for a kiss on the lips. His affectionate movements mirrored a scene Kirby had witnessed between Clothiste and Etienne while on his sojourn to colonial times.

I guess PDA runs in the family.

The fond interaction between Stephanie and Gage punched at Kirby's gut. He had thought he and Sandi were heading for the same kind of relationship.

Until the text with those four words.

"Is this the proverbial pregnant pause?" a voice asked in his ear.

Jumping in surprise, Kirby whirled to face Kyle Avery, the former history professor who had recently become engaged to Terry.

"What?" Kirby nearly shouted. *Geez, man, poor choice of words.*

"Hey, man, sorry to scare you. I couldn't get into the dining room with all the PDA going on between the fireman and his girl, so I came to this door and found you lost in thought." Kyle carried a small cooler and he flipped the lid. "Want a beer?"

"No, I'm good." Kirby's heart still thudded at the word "pregnant."

"Well, I want one. I have a feeling the spirits will be flowing if we are gonna get through this night."

"I'm all up for facing spirits," Chase Hallmark said as he followed Kyle into the room. He carried a large bottle of whiskey and raised it up. "This kind, not the ethereal kind."

"Get in here, you idiots," Terry called. "You sound like a bunch of booze hounds."

Chase, Mary Jo's fiancé and longtime Dunbar family friend, smirked. "You ladies can have that sissy grape. We'll have the real stuff." He nudged Kirby forward.

As he stepped toward the table, Kirby's gaze swept the room. Stephanie edged close to his side and slipped her arm in the crook of his. "She's coming, Kirby. She went to check on Margaret. She said the poor little girl fell into such a deep sleep that she's checked one her twice already."

Kirby nodded, and greeted the other three men in the room. He tried to shake the feeling of impending doom that formed an acid pit deep in his stomach. Kyle had no way of knowing his innocent joke had sent Kirby into a tailspin.

How am I going to break the news to Sandi that Liana is pregnant? His gut tightened, and he could barely discern the conversation around him.

"Where did you get the whiskey from?" Gage asked. "I've never seen that label." He turned the bottle over and read the name on the label out loud. "Clan McGowan?"

"It's a new craft whiskey. The distiller, Skyler McGowan, is planning to open a distillery and distribution center right here in Olde Towne. And guess *who* got the remodeling job?"

"Hallmark Construction, of course." Mary Jo and Stephanie said in unison.

Chase beamed at them, pride lighting his usually stoic face. "I've been able to hire another full crew." Following the aftermath of Hurricane Abigail, Chase's small construction firm had gained a reputation for quality work in a timely manner and at affordable prices. His foremen could barely keep up with the new jobs rolling in.

"Is Kevin still working weekends with you?" Terry asked.

"Every chance he gets." Chase opened the bottle of Scottish spirits and set it aside. He wagged his finger at Terry. "And he's getting minimum wage, Miss Fair Labor Standards Act."

Terry laughed. At Kirby's blank look, she explained, "It's a running joke. Kevin was one of three teenagers that were involved in several acts of vandalism during the remodeling of Clothiste's Inn. Rather than charge the boys with crimes, we worked out an agreement with their parents to assist Chase in the repairs until they paid off the costs of the damage. Kevin had taken to carpentry like the proverbial duck to water. Even after he met his obligation, he continued to help, so Chase has let him work odd jobs to earn a little money. He has retained me to represent him in the event Hallmark Construction fails to pay him minimum wages."

"More like you hired yourself, ambulance-chaser," Chase teased. Terry crumbled a napkin and tossed it at him.

Kirby nodded, frown lines creasing his forehead.

"Hey, Kirby, don't look so down." Chase clamped his hand on Kirby's shoulder. "I'll hire you to work for me."

The small group broke into laughter just as Sandi entered the room. Kirby swallowed and shifted with guilt.

"Whose hiring whom and what did I miss?" she asked, glancing toward the darkened parlor. Worry lined her face.

Terry put her arm around Sandi. "No signs of any activity in there," she said.

"I know. But I have to take a look first."

"I'll go with you," Terry offered. She kept her arm tight around her law partner's shoulder as they walked toward the fireplace in the parlor.

In the mirror above the colonial-style mantel, their reflections were a normal image.

"Norrie, can you hear me?" Sandi touched the glass. Her fingertips met against the reflection, the surface solid to her touch. She tapped her nails in light clicks, then racked her knuckles hard against the glass.

Silence greeted the women.

"Where is she, Terry?" Sandi's voice wavered.

"I don't know, Sandi, but try not to worry. You and Kirby made it back to our time safely. Whatever wires crossed that put Norrie where she is and sent Maggie to us must need a significant event to work things out. We will find the answer. Norrie is a resilient little girl and Maggie doesn't seem to be all the worse for her ordeals in time travel."

Sandi pressed her hand to her stomach. "It's just so awful, not knowing."

"If anyone can figure out what to do, it will be those two ancestry sleuths Stephanie and Kyle." Terry inclined her head toward the dining room.

"I know, but, Terry, we're lawyers. We deal in facts and hard evidence, not the unknown. What would people think if they knew we stood in front of a mirror waiting for it to become a time portal?"

The attorneys looked at each other and broke into quiet giggles.

"All of our clients would run away, we'd be disbarred and sent to the loony bin, that's for sure. Now let's go eat while we brainstorm with the others."

***

Liana headed to Portsmouth. Not seeing Kirby's car parked at his darkened apartment, Liana next drove toward Clothiste's Inn. She located Kirby's vehicle in the rear lot of the business, with five or six other cars nearby. She exited the parking lot and circled the block until she found a parking space on the street in front of the B and B. She saw movement and eased from the driver's seat.

She never understood Kirby's fascination for that place—or the French pastry shop beside it. *Pâtisseries a la Carte* was a cute little bistro, but she preferred more modern places that served vegetarian and health foods.

Liana walked up the steps to the wraparound porch and peered into the window. Two women stood with their backs to her. A small table lamp illuminated the room, and she recognized Terry reaching down to turn out the light. A crystal chandelier illuminated the dining room beyond, its brightness temporarily blocked as the two figures walked from the dark parlor and walked toward the dining room table.

Kirby held the chair out for one of the women, then he sat beside her. They shared a quick kiss.

His lawyer lady. Liana sneered. Then someone stepped into the archway of the door separating the dining room and the parlor, blocking her view.

She stepped away from the window and pressed her back against the house. Anger turned into a full fury that left her quaking. Closing her eyes, she clenched her jaw.

How dare he act as if nothing had happened! She took out her cell phone and dialed. When his voice message kicked in, she bit back her rage and spoke in a quiet, civil tone.

"Kirby, honey, you have every right to be angry with me for the affair with Spencer, but I regret it and want to be with you. Please call me at this number and let's talk. I love you." She clicked the disconnect button.

"You bastard," she spat as she shoved the phone into her purse.

When she had her composure under control, she took another glance through the window and stopped short.

Icy fingers of cold trickled down her collar and her heart thumped wildly.

While she gazed into the same window, the scene before her had changed. The rooms were lit by candles flickering in wall sconces and in candelabra on the fireplace mantel and on tables.

Reminiscent of an elegant party scene of *Gone with The Wind*, women in hoop-skirt gowns and men in fashionable vests under cutaway coats filled the room. When the sea of bodies parted, Liana had a clear view into the dining room.

Guests seated at the table were not the same ones she had just observed.

She gasped and leaned back against the house, fingernails scraping the siding as she clawed in fear. A cold chill replaced the heat of anger, and she shivered.

Drawing her coat tighter, she glanced through the window again.

Modern-day couples gathered at the dining table, mouths moving in inaudible conversation.

How long have I been standing here? Liana pressed her knuckles to her mouth and shook her head.

She'd been told she was crazy before.

Maybe it was true after all.

CHAPTER 2

Portsmouth, Virginia
1861

Daniel and Lauralee took a break from dancing to greet his cousin Celestine and her husband Frank.

"What a wonderful party this is," Lauralee gushed.

"You and Frank are wonderful hosts," Daniel said. "I am so glad we were able to make the trip this year."

"We are delighted that you are here, Cousin Daniel," Celestine said. "You need to relax more often."

"I tell him that all the time, Celestine. And I suspect he is about to ensnare your husband with talk of the troubles between the North and the South."

"Then we shall have a refreshing drink while they discuss business." Celestine linked her arm with Lauralee's and led her toward the punchbowl while Daniel and Frank stepped onto the veranda.

Upstairs, the scullery maid stopped abruptly as the floor squeaked under her plain, flat shoes, and she darted into a shadowy corner. Beads of perspiration lined her forehead in the humid summer night.

Laughter and voices drifted upward, more discernible after the musicians stopped, as the party guests continued to talk in the same volume as before the music ended.

The band struck up the tune of a lively reel, and footfalls of dancers added to the sounds below. Any noise she made would not be noticed by the partygoers.

She sighed in relief. She was supposed to be working in the outside kitchen, but the cooks had sent her to the main house with supper for the old woman. She had taken the food upstairs, where the nurse snatched the tray from her hands and summarily dismissed her without even a thank-you.

The maid glared as the door slammed shut in her face.

How dare she look down on me? Who does she think she is?

Resentment coursed through her as the song ended and the dancers burst into applause. She belonged with those people, not skulking like a frightened rabbit in servant's clothes. How easy the other girls have it, tending to the guests, while she was nothing more than a scullery maid.

She glanced in the other bedrooms, filled with the belongings of overnight guests. Unable to resist, she stepped over the threshold and picked up a lace shawl draped over the footboard of the canopy bed. She ran her fingers over the intricate pattern and stopped short when her gaze drifted to a small brass box on a table beside the bed.

A loud gasp escaped her lips when she lifted the lid, revealing two velvet-lined trays holding a treasure trove of gold, silver, and precious gems. The bottom tray held two necklaces with matching earrings, with an empty space where a third set would go—probably being worn by a guest downstairs.

She may have been poor, but she knew jewels, often studying the ones displayed in the window of Ferguson's Jewelers until the crotchety old man would chase her away.

The maid wasted no time. She tied the ends of her apron to the waistband to form a pouch into which she emptied the contents of the box. Her heart rocked against her breastbone as she replaced the lid.

After a quick glance over her shoulder, she eased open the small drawer in the table to reveal a number of items. A pair of gold cufflinks engraved with an ornate letter "M" nestled beside black wire-rimmed glasses on a linen handkerchief embroidered with a similar royal blue "M" in one corner.

She scooped the cufflinks into her apron. Underneath the handkerchief, she found a bone-handled pistol. She picked the gun up and slid her finger over the "M" carved in the handle in the same design as the cufflinks and handkerchief.

She added the firearm to her collection and bolted from the room.

As she pressed her back against the wall, the pounding in her chest echoed in her ears. She peeked around the hallway. The door to the old woman's room remained closed. She skirted around the ornate banister and practically flew down the stairs.

What if someone caught her with the jewelry?

She managed to leave the building without running into the homeowner, guest, or any of the staff. Unaware she had been holding her breath, she expelled air from her longs. Cradling the treasure in her apron with one hand, she gathered her skirts and ran into the yard, past the outside kitchen where the cook staff toiled.

Without a second glance she raced in the opposite direction to hide until she could figure out what to do.

Modern Day Portsmouth, Virginia

"This is quite an international feast," Stephanie remarked as she looked around. Italian food from Antonio's, German *rouladen* and the schnitzel bites from the nearby Bier Haus, chicken wings and fried pickles from the Sports Bar filled the plates of the four couples seated at the table. Three-tiered pedestal stands loaded with Mary Jo's French pastries lined the buffet.

"I like a mix of tastes like this. International in Olde Towne works for me," Gage said as he reached for a platter of bite-sized chicken schnitzel pieces.

The room grew silent, broken only by the occasional clink of glass or tap of silverware as the four couples dined.

Despite his hunger, Kirby had no appetite for the smorgasbord on the table. Anxiety burned the very pit of his stomach. He pushed a slice of lasagna around the plate.

"I guess I should be the first to talk about the elephant in the room," he declared. Concern for the two little girls who were lost in time and Liana's disturbing message continued to churn his gut. Eyes turned in his direction. He avoided looking at Sandi. *Well, we can talk about one elephant, anyway.*

"I'm assuming before everyone got here that the women have brought you guys up to speed as far as they could?"

He glanced around at Chase, Gage, and Kyle, who nodded.

"Fantastic as it seems," Chase muttered. Mary Jo tapped her elbow into his side.

"Wait, let me grab my pen and paper." Stephanie, the consummate notetaker, jumped to her feet and retrieved the items.

"Stephanie and her lists," Terry said, rolling her eyes skyward.

"Hey, that's my woman you are complaining about," Gage said. "And her notes have solved a lot of family mysteries." He put his arm around his fiancée, who stuck her tongue out at his sister.

"Oh, don't get bent out of shape, bro," Terry said. She flicked her fingers under her chin toward Stephanie. "I was just joking."

"I know," Stephanie said with a giggle.

Kirby cleared his throat and waited for the sibling conflict to die down. "I know this all sounds implausible. Hell, I'm a medical man. Nothing in medical school ever prepared me for anything like this." He poked at the lasagna again. "But we can better analyze this if I start from the beginning. We know the common connection we all have is that we are descendants of the children of Étienne and his wife Clothiste. The other common connection is that we each inherited a jewel that once belonged to those same children." Kirby turned his hand palm downward, displaying the emerald ring on his left ring finger to the others.

In unison the three named women touched their fingers to heirloom pendants at their necks. Stephanie wore a teardrop-shaped diamond, Mary Jo a ruby heart, and Terry a gold cross with a sapphire at the intersection of the two bars.

"We were each haunted by the ghost of our colonial ancestor to find their missing jewels, which also led us to solve the mystery of whose bones were buried in the backyard," Stephanie added.

Kirby nodded. "But the brother, Louis, was trapped between life and death, burdened by the guilt of a crime he thought he committed. I first saw his image the night of the party that celebrated the grand opening of Clothiste's Inn, remember? Then I saw it again, the first night I stayed at the inn as a guest. I came into the parlor at the stroke of midnight, just in time to see the image fade and then I faced Sandi with her gun aimed at my heart."

Heads swiveled in Sandi's direction and she shrugged. "I've been carrying ever since Shady O'Grady attacked Terry."

"Might want to make a mental note that these are four

ladies who can take care of themselves," Kyle added. He placed his hand over Terry's and gave a small squeeze before continuing. "So, tell us what happened next, Kirby."

"Well, the next day I went to Busch Gardens with Sandi and Norrie. We got home late and went straight to our rooms. I woke up because I heard a child crying and came downstairs to investigate. Nothing was amiss downstairs and I heard nothing from Sandi's room."

Sandi nodded. "I heard crying as well, but Norrie was fast asleep."

Kirby continued. "I went to the parlor and stood in front of the fireplace just as the clock was clicking toward midnight. On the first chime, the candlesticks jumped around, the hands of the clock spun backwards, the room started to glow, and I saw Louis in the mirror. It was as if he stood at a waterfall."

He glanced around the table, expecting to see faces of skepticism. Too much supernatural had recently occurred to his family and friends, and he found the audience listened with accepting ears.

"Thanks for giving me the benefit of the doubt and not looking at me like I'm crazy." Kirby laughed, but his smile did not reach his eyes. "In the middle of all that weird shimmering shit, Louis then reached for me and pulled me into the mirror. I spun around in the dark. Man, my skin stretched over my bones, and I thought it was going to rip away." In an absent-minded gesture, he swiped his hand along his jaw as if pushing his skin back in place.

Sandi leaned forward. "Meantime, I had had a bad dream where I was looking for Norrie, and running down long corridors of doors. I woke up to find her safe beside me. I went to use the bathroom and heard the childlike crying again. I rushed from the bathroom and saw that Norrie was gone from the bed. I found her in the living room, staring at the clock. She walked toward it, I think it was about the third or toll fourth chiming in these long, drawn-out gongs. I grabbed her and we were swept into this kind of wind tunnel. We just spun in the air, almost floating until we landed. We had nothing like the painful experiences Kirby had." She squeezed his hand.

Kirby nodded. "I landed on my butt in the bedroom of a home with a lot of activity going on. I soon came to realize I was witnessing Étienne and Clothiste, perhaps only minutes after Louis was born. I could see them, every detail of the room. No one could see me. It was as if I were the ghost and they were living. But I was solid, I could feel things, smell things. They spoke French, but somehow, I became an expert at understanding them even though I have never studied the language. But no one saw me or heard my rather noisy arrival. They discussed naming Louis after Clothiste's father and what they hoped for his future. Then, far away I heard the toll of a bell, and I swear Clothiste looked at me right then but I was swept away again. I soon learned that whenever a clock struck the hour somewhere near me, I was sent into another period of Louis and his family's lives. The next time was when he was a little boy. His resemblance to Tanner was uncanny." Tanner was the young son of Gage and Terry's younger brother Connor.

"Tanner was certainly the lightning rod for all of our ancestors to contact each of us," Stephanie said. Mary Jo and Terry nodded.

"But Tanner wasn't with Kirby when he had this experience," Chase pointed out.

"I don't think that he was needed anymore by that time." Kyle poured a glass of wine and leaned back. He

22

settled his eyeglasses on his nose, his face an uncanny resemblance to a young Harrison Ford playing Indiana Jones. "Tanner helped the sisters cross over that barrier, from the limbo of the world they were trapped in, to the point where they made the contact with their descendants to find their missing necklaces and solve the mysteries. They needed the help to find the lost jewels and fulfill their destiny in order to pass to their afterlife. Kirby already had the ring in his possession, passed down as a family heirloom."

"Don't forget that Tanner was with me the very first night I saw the image in the mirror," Kirby said. "Remember, I dressed in a British redcoat costume? He was unhappy about having to dress as a drummer boy. I had picked him up and we were looking at the mirror. Tanner saluted and said 'aye, aye, sir,' and even though he was talking to me, he was looking right at the mirror. In fact, I now believe we saw Louis' face and not mine in the reflection. So, I guess we could say he facilitated my contact as well."

"All right then, what happened after you—went back?" Chase asked. He stumbled over the phrase, his grimace revealing the mixed emotions of uncertainty and objectivity.

Kirby blew his breath in a huff. "Where to begin? I got swept from this birth scene to a few years later, at Christmas time, with the family. Marie Josephé was just a small baby, sleeping through the festivities. Louis had received a drum, and Theresé a doll, which I believe is the same one you found hidden in the attic during the hurricane, Stephanie."

With a resigned shrug, he leaned back in his chair before continuing. "Every time a bell rang, I got sent somewhere else. I even made a joke about that scene from the Christmas movie, which of course no one of that period understood. You know, the movie where Clarence the Angel gets his wings?"

"*It's a Wonderful Life*," Stephanie interjected. Around the table, heads bobbed in agreement.

Kirby also nodded, repeating the title once before continuing his story. "I'm glad the travel Sandi and Norrie experienced did not cause them the pain I endured. Each time I transitioned from one scene to the next, the journey became more painful than the previous."

No one in the room moved or spoke, wide eyes riveted on Kirby.

He continued with a slight lift of his shoulders. "I twisted and turned through dark vortexes. My skin stretched beyond belief, my body elongated until I thought I would snap. Lights flashed, and I twirled so hard, I didn't know if I was coming or going, whether I was face up or face down."

Kirby reached for his glass and took a sip. "I saw Louis as a young man in Williamsburg, meeting George Washington, and…"

"Wait, you saw George Washington?" Kyle interrupted. The former college history professor's jaw dropped at Kirby's nod of affirmation.

"And Cornwallis as well, Kyle. But more about that later. I suffered a temporary hearing loss from a dunk in an icy river and could not hear the discussion, but Étienne had presented Louis to Washington at Christiana Campbell's Tavern. The real, absolute original, decked out for Christmas tavern, with Madame Campbell herself serving the good general. The best I could determine is that Washington had accepted Louis into service. When father and son left the tavern, Étienne gave Louis the emerald ring."

He held up his hand. The green stone glistened in the beams of the chandelier but emitted none of the vibes he'd often experienced prior to his time travel.

Kirby shoved his chair back from the table and stood. "You all go on eating. I've got to move around the room a bit."

He walked to the sideboard and fingered the neck of the whiskey bottle, then poured a good amount into a tumbler. He gulped it down, letting the fiery liquid sear his throat.

Kirby poured another shot, but set the glass down. "Then on another time travel, I met Maggie. I had no idea she was a child of time, not of the eighteenth century. I learned Abigail had forced the little girl into servitude after dismissing Lizzie, the maid who was also a spy and whom Louis eventually married. Louis arranged for Lizzie to escape, and she insisted on taking Maggie with her."

"We know from our research that Lizzie was Abigail's niece, indentured to repay to a debt her mother incurred. Abigail was a very powerful woman for her time, Kirby," Stephanie said as she walked to his side. "She made life miserable, especially for Clothiste and the three daughters. And Lizzie as well."

"After seeing them safely on their way, Louis came back to the house and found his mother at the foot of the stairs, near death."

"I witnessed that scene when Clothiste fell down the stairs," Terry said.

The eyes of the males in the room widened in amazement.

She shrugged. "I didn't tell anyone, except for Stephanie and Mary Jo, and later Sandi. It was too crazy. But yes, I had a time travel experience during one of

Theresé's visits. She had materialized into human form, and we were standing in the parlor. The clock went crazy, I remember that, but we didn't travel through a time tunnel or vortex, or anything like that. It was as if Theresé and I simply floated to the ceiling while the scene changed below us. We were suddenly in the upstairs hall of this very house, except we were in colonial times. A violent storm raged outside. From our position, we observed the fight between Abigail and Clothiste. One of Clothiste's arms was injured, apparently from when she was shot, but she managed a couple of good licks with the silver candlestick." She flicked her gaze toward the parlor where the antique candlesticks stood. "She and Abigail clawed at each other, bouncing from wall to wall, until Clothiste slipped and tumbled down the stairs. Abigail regained her balance, but her foot slipped and she crumbled at the top of the stairs, one leg bent under her in a grotesque injury."

"I did not see any of that happen." Kirby rolled the empty glass between his palms. He set it down with a hard thump. "After Louis had come to take Lizzie and little Margaret away. I followed them until he got them on their way, then he raced back to his grandfather's house. I was right behind him. We must have arrived just after Abigail and Clothiste had fought. His mother lay crumpled at the foot of the steps, bleeding and hardly breathing. She managed to gasp that Abigail had tried to kill Phillip. Louis thought she had died in his arms, and he left her to go upstairs, but she was still alive—barely—when I got to her. With her last breath she begged me to help him. She told me she knew I would come."

Silence followed his words. A tear slid down Stephanie's cheek and she stood. She walked beside Kirby, patted his arm, then poured a shot of Clan

McGowan. She belted it back and gasped, spraying the contents as they burned her throat.

"Oh, my word, how can anyone drink that?" she sputtered.

"You can't, you're French," teased Chase. The playful remark broke some of the somber atmosphere of the room.

Kirby smiled. "Funny you should say that. I will tell you later about several lively discussions I was involved in about wine versus scotch, but let me finish this first. After Clothiste died, I raced up the stairs to find Abigail sprawled at the top of the stars, badly injured. Louis was tending to his grandfather in one of the bedrooms, running between rooms to get supplies."

"Theresé told me that Louis never got over the guilt of killing Abigail," Terry said.

"But in reality, he didn't kill her. That guilt haunted him his whole life and prevented him from dying in peace. He was trapped in time, existing in a void that held him prisoner over one hundred and fifty years." Kirby returned to his seat. "Oh, he had every intention of doing so when he pressed his hands along her windpipe and squeezed. He didn't know that she was still alive when he left her to go to his grandfather, but she did die on the steps. While I knelt beside her, Louis finally came back to kneel beside her one more time, and it was that point that we made eye contact. He reached for me and asked for help. Eerie green sparks shot out between our rings. The clock chimed and took me away before I could say anything." His eyes took on a faraway look as he turned his hand palm upward and stretched, as if reaching for a hand.

"So maybe Louis' guilt caused him to somehow become trapped in time, between life and death but somewhere between our world and his?" Kyle's matter-of-fact professor's voice matched Kirby's calm tone. "Not a ghost like his sisters, whose spirits were able to enter our world. He was entombed in time. It wasn't until everything came together at the right moment that he could be free—Kirby's presence here in this house, with the emerald ring, at the right stroke of midnight on the antique clock."

"It's how I figured it," Kirby said.

"So how did Maggie get caught up in this?" Stephanie asked. "Could she tell you anything, Sandi?"

"Not really. I talked with her before she fell asleep, to make sure she was all right." Sandi sighed. "She seems to be taking all this time travel in stride, considering she lived in the nineteenth century and somehow was sent to the eighteenth. And now she's here in the twenty-first. She told me that she remembers playing hide-and-seek with her brothers. She hid in the magnolia tree and could hear them calling for her, but she wouldn't come out because they had teased her so much. When a storm came up and it began to thunder and lightning, she got caught in the tree and ran into the alley. A wagon rumbled by and someone grabbed her as it passed. She said a man and lady argued and there was a gun. Maggie fell asleep. When she woke up, she was in a different house, very run down and dirty. The first lady was nowhere in sight. Another older lady was in a carriage, and the man made her go with the woman."

Kirby nodded. "She said big winds picked up the wagon and a mean man sold her to a woman. Apparently, she had landed in colonial Richmond when Abigail had come to purchase a servant. Maggie has certainly adapted well. We had no idea she was not a colonial child. She played with the other kids and did chores, never once indicating she was out of place, until the moment she told Sandi and I her father had taken her to see the president. We were at the surrender at Yorktown. Washington was not yet president, we were confused and asked her if she meant President Washington. She said 'No, silly, President Lincoln.' And that's about the time we got sent back here."

"Wait, now. The surrender at Yorktown? How did Lincoln get involved?" Kyle asked.

Kirby gave a helpless shrug. "He didn't. We said we were witnessing history in the making and she said her father said that when they went to see Lincoln and that was our first clue. But let me finish Louis' story. After his grandfather died, Louis buried Abigail under the spindling magnolia tree—also a common denominator linking the past and present. Louis hid in the outside kitchen, trying to figure out how to handle everything and not get charged with murder. Therese arrived, not knowing yet about their mother's death, so they devised a plan. Unfortunately for me, that was when my next time warp brought me into the picture. I arrived just as Therese was about to whack Louis with a board, intending to tell everyone that robbers had attacked and rendered him unconscious. I took the brunt of the hit and woke up beside Louis in prison." Kirby looked up. "Did any of you know that while Benedict Arnold was in Portsmouth, he converted a sugar warehouse into a prison?"

Only the history professor nodded. The others shook their heads.

"Well, that's where I landed next, in the sugar warehouse turned prison. The situation was appalling. American prisoners of war were in squalid conditions, sick, starving. The guards were inhumane. By this time, I was no longer invisible to everyone around me. The Brits suspected Louis was a spy, which he was, but my arrival and nearly identical look gave him an alibi that it was I who was the spy. He was released. I am sure one of the guards had it in for me, but fortunately, my time travel whisked me out of there, just in the nick of time."

The others groaned and Kirby gave an apologetic shrug. "I eventually landed in the middle of the Yorktown battlefield. Cannons boomed and soldiers fell dead, one right on top of me. A little French boy was helping the gunner, and Marie Josephé came to help. I did what I could to help her and the boy manning the cannon. There was a lot of carnage around us."

Mary Jo gave a start, knocking over her empty wine glass. The former Army soldier had listened closely but had remained silent through Kirby's tale. She turned wide eyes to him.

"Oh, my god, I used to have a dream like that all the time, where I was on a Revolutionary War battlefield helping man the cannon. Like Molly Pitcher or something. Sometimes it changed to a modern army battle scene like when I was in Afghanistan, although the colonial scenes were always more vivid."

"Well, you are descended from Marie Josephé, who wanted to fight the Brits even though she was a girl. Remember? I found Clothiste's diary during Hurricane Abby. It revealed a lot to us," Stephanie pointed out.

"It's just all too weird for me," Mary Jo said with a shake of her head. "If I had not had my own encounters with Marie Josephé I would have called the men in white coats on y'all a long time ago."

The mantel clock chimed. Kirby glanced at his watch.

"Ten o'clock."

Sandi stiffened and jumped from her chair. She raced to the parlor. As she had done every previous sixty minutes, she stood in front of the innocuous clock as it counted the hour. Kirby joined her and they stood close as the ten bells tolled.

The soft light from the dining room chandelier provided the only illumination in the quiet, still room.

***

Through the window pane, the muffled chimes of a clock reached Liana's ears. She glanced back through the window and glared at Kirby and Sandi embracing. A woman walked into the parlor and turned on a low table lamp before walking toward the couple. All three stared at the mirror over the fireplace.

Recognizing Terry, Liana shrank into the shadows. She disliked Sandi's law partner, one of the few women she'd ever met who intimidated her. Her breath formed a frosty cloud as she seethed when Kirby wrapped his arm around Sandi's shoulders. Kirby's lady lawyer pressed her face into his chest, her body racking with sobs. He gathered her closer.

"I'll give you something to cry about, bitch," she muttered as she backed away from the window.

***

The tenth toll reverberated and the parlor fell into silence.

Terry tugged Sandi's sleeve. "It still wasn't the right time, Sandi. It will come."

"I don't know what I was expecting," Sandi said with a sigh as they walked to the dining room where Stephanie and Gage cleared dishes. Chase put away beverages while Kyle gathered stemware. "We don't have the first indication of what needs to be done to change the girls back to their own times."

"Sandi, I think whatever needs to happen is going to be associated with three o'clock, since that was the hour that returned you to our time." Stephanie paused in the middle of transferring food from casserole dishes to smaller storage containers and waved a spoon in the air. "Whether that is a.m. or p.m., I can't tell you. But I am going to read through all the family journals and letters again, see if anything can give me a clue."

"And Kyle and I will be staying at my apartment so we are only a phone call away," Terry said. She owned the building next door that housed her and Sandi's law firm on the ground floor, with a two-bedroom on the second floor that she used when she needed to stay overnight in Olde Towne.

"Thank you, all of you. Norrie and I don't have any family near us, so your support means a lot." Sandi picked up dishes and shot a worried glance at Kirby's nearly-full plate.

"Kirby, you didn't eat anything."

"I managed a little. I think my body's been through too much to eat right."

Mary Jo brought a pot of coffee to the table. "This is decaf, gang. We don't need a caffeine overload at this time of night. Sandi, earlier tonight when we went to get the food, Chase and I decided we would spend the night in the inn. We brought overnight bags. I say we load the dishwasher and get a good night's sleep." She held her hand up as Sandi started to speak. "And, yes, Sandi, I doubt any of us will get much sleep and we will be down here at three in the morning—just in case."

"I'm so thankful to have all of you helping me," Sandi said. "I know we will get through this, somehow."

The coffee pot remained untouched. The four young couples said goodnights and retired for the night, no closer to a solution on how to return two lost girls to their own time than they were before dinner.

And with no clue of the devious plans brewing in the mind of an unsettled woman.

CHAPTER 3

Portsmouth Virginia 1861

"How awful. Poor Cousin Celestine!" Lauralee stared into the mirror as she brushed her hair.

Her husband Daniel caught her eye and gave a nod. He sat on the edge of the bed as his young daughter stood on tiptoes to comb his hair.

"They immediately reported the theft when they discovered it this morning, but the maid they suspect has not been seen since she brought a tray upstairs to Celestine's great-grandmama Theresé." His head jerked backwards. "And darling daughter Margaret, must you rake your comb through my scalp as if you are tending a garden?"

Margaret giggled. "Papa, you are so funny. You make me laugh. And I like that you call me Margaret instead of Maggie. I hate my nickname."

She skipped to her mother's dressing table and ran the comb through her mother's honey-brown curls. "Mama, why must you wear your hair pinned up most days? It is so pretty and I love the curls like you wear today. I wish my hair was like yours."

"It is usually much too hot to wear it down, and your hair is lovely just the way it is. Would you like me to braid it for you?"

"Yes, please, Mama. Will you tie the braids with my ribbons? Why did the lady take the jewelry?"

"No one knows for sure who took them or why, but they suspect the maid." Lauralee turned her daughter around and with deft fingers created two braids.

"What will they do to her when they find her?" Margaret handed her mother a slash of ribbon.

"She will have to answer to the police and probably go to prison."

"Will she stay there forever?" Margaret angled her head to study the finished hairdo.

"My goodness, little one, you are full of questions!" Daniel kissed the top of his daughter's head and stood beside his wife. He caught her gaze in the mirror again and gave her a flirty little wink. Twin blushes appeared on Lauralee's cheeks, but she smiled.

He leaned close to her ear and whispered, "And how pleased I am that my winks can still make my wife blush."

Lauralee waved a lace handkerchief at Daniel. "Behave yourself." She batted her eyes above a second, coyer smile. Then she frowned. "Well, the thief—or thieves—did not find their way here to our room. I should have been quite angry to lose my lovely jewels that you worked so hard to give me."

"Speaking of jewels, I must take my ring off." Daniel slipped a gold band from his finger and touched the emerald at the crown. "I snagged it on my vest when I was taking out my pocket watch, and caused a prong to bend. Now the stone is loose."

"Oh, my. I too have a jewelry calamity." Lauralee reached into a drawer to withdraw a small velvet bag. She shook the cloth and a brooch watch fell into her palm. A loose chain slid out as well. "The clasp of my beloved pearl watch necklace has broken. I can still wear it pinned on as a brooch, but I have put it aside for safekeeping. Wrap your ring in a handkerchief and I will put it in my pouch. When we get back home, we can have Mr. Ferguson repair them for us."

Daniel pulled a white linen handkerchief from his pocket and placed the ring in the creases, folding until he had formed a small square pocket. Lauralee took it from him and put it in the pouch. He brushed her lips with a kiss, and with one hand she absentmindedly set the bag beside her perfume bottle as she drew her husband closer for a deeper kiss.

Maggie giggled and tinkered with the pretty items on the dressing table. She moved a small hand mirror to one side and pushed a powder box toward a perfume bottle. Then she used the silver-handled comb to run through her tresses, all the while eyeing the image of her mother's back in the mirror.

Her Aunt Celestine came to the bedroom door. Her eyes were red-rimmed from crying.

"Any news of the thief, Celestine dear?" Lauralee rose and crossed the floor to greet her husband's cousin with a kiss on the cheek.

"Nothing. It is as if she vanished. Or never existed. We have decided to continue with the garden party today. Will you join me?"

"Of course." Lauralee stepped into the hall, then called over her shoulder. "Come along, Maggie. The children will be arriving for games."

"Yes, Mama." Maggie slid from the seat, watching her mother's back in the mirror. Her gaze drifted to the bag.

Do little girls go to prison for taking things?

A moment later, she snatched the velvet pouch and stuffed it in the pocket of her pinafore before she skipped to catch up to her mother.

Modern Day Portsmouth, Virginia

Two more days passed since Kirby, Sandi, and Margaret had returned from the time warp.

Although the law office was only next door, Sandi refused to leave the inn for long periods. She brought work from her office to her room, and handled calls on her cell phone, but no matter what she was doing, she made a point to be standing in front of the mirror at three, both morning and afternoon.

Margaret remained close by Sandi's side. She shied away from the television, and covered her eyes when it came on, so Sandi got her news from the internet rather than TV. Sometimes when Margaret played with Norrie's doll, she would pause and ask where the other child was.

Sandi struggled to explain. "Norrie is traveling in…" She paused. *How to explain time travel to the child when I don't even understand it myself?* "Remember the lights in the strange tunnel we were in, where it seemed like we were floating on air, and then we came through a door?"

Margaret nodded, tightening her grip on Norrie's doll.

"Well, it is something strange that happened and I can't really explain it. I think that Norrie traveled through the air, in the same odd way that you and I and Kirby did, but somehow, she went through a different door. We don't know where she is, but we think she may be at your home, waiting for us to find her. We have to try to get you back to your family and bring Norrie home with us."

"Is she trapped in the box like those people?" Margaret pointed to the small TV nearby.

"Well, not exactly, honey," Sandi said, turning to Kirby for help.

"We don't know how it happens, Margret," Kirby offered. "It has something to do with time, where it moves people from the place they are supposed to be to another place."

Tears welled in Margaret's eyes. "I want to go home. I've been gone ever so long, and I miss Mama and Papa. They will be so angry with me. I dropped Papa's ring and it got broked. And I lost-ed Mama's watch with the pearls

37

too. I had it when the man and lady took me in the wagon but I fell asleep. When I woke up, I was at the mean lady's house. She made me clean and do laundry."

Kirby's phone rang and his muscles stiffened before he glanced at the screen. His caller ID showed Stephanie's number. Relieved, he answered.

"Hi, Kirby." Stephanie's voice sounded rushed. "Weather reports indicate severe thunderstorms are headed our way this evening. You know how storms seem to coincide with our mysteries. Maybe we should plan something. Can you meet at the Bier Haus at two? Tanner and his parents are coming by. I wanted to include them, in case Tanner can help, but Beth won't bring him to the inn."

He repeated the message to Sandi, who shook her head as she tapped her watch.

"Let's wait until five," Kirby suggested to Stephanie as Sandi nodded. "Sandi will want to be here at three anyway, and I need to take care of some business." Pressing the cell phone against his chest, Kirby whispered, "Sandi, you have to get out of here for a while. We can be back here in a flash, every hour if you want. Please."

"Can we just meet at the café tonight? I know they won't be open, but I just can't go too far away yet," she asked.

Kirby relayed the question to Stephanie. Apparently, Mary Jo stood nearby as Stephanie's muffled voice repeated the request. She came back to the line and said, "Yes, Beth says Tanner can go to the café, but we'll have to order something from outside. We had a banner day here at the café and other than a few croissants, we have very little left."

"We're fine with anything. Thank you."

"All right, I will let the others know. See you at five."

Kirby hung up and turned to Sandi, who chewed on her bottom lip with worry.

She said, "Do you think Maggie will be okay if we leave the house? She has barely left my side, and we haven't even stepped outside since we arrived."

"I don't know what to expect, Sandi. Look, now don't get angry at me, but your life is going to have to move on soon. We have no way of knowing how long this is going to take, or how to be in the right place at the right time to bring Norrie home." *If we even can.*

"If we even can," Sandi echoed, as if reading the words in his mind. "We may never get her back, Kirby. Look how long Maggie has been gone from her time."

"I know, babe, I know. But try to think of it this way. Maggie seems able to adjust well, and she's been through three time periods now. We spent weeks and months in colonial times, yet when we returned home, we'd only been gone less than a day. If things work out the way Kyle thinks they might, Maggie will return home to her own time period, and Norrie will return here with us, and it will be just a few days after she left."

"Thank God you are with me through this, Kirby. Will life ever get straight again? It is a hell of a way to begin a relationship, isn't it?" Tears spilled down Sandi's cheeks. Kirby drew her into his arms and let her weep into his shoulder.

That's not the half of it. He closed his eyes. Those four words of Liana's text message burned into his brain. "Call me, I'm pregnant." Although he had tried to contact her several times she had not answered and did not have a voice mail set up for this new number. He needed to meet with her to get their lives sorted out.

Sandi sniffled and Kirby handed her his handkerchief.

She blew her nose, and when she spoke, her voice held the nasal pitch of tears. "Maybe after we find Norrie, we can see where this goes."

He nodded but didn't speak.

Finding Norrie is going to be the easy part.

***

Overcast skies grew darker and more ominous as the afternoon light faded. Kirby turned on a table light and went back to his laptop. He perused an offer from one of the civilian medical teams with whom he had interviewed, but he could not concentrate on the details.

He had wanted to tell Sandi about Liana's message right away, but the worry over Norrie's disappearance took all of their immediate concentration. And he needed to contact Liana before he discussed it with Sandi anyway. Pulling out his cell phone, he listened to Liana's last message again, her voice dripping with a honey-sweet serenity that sent icicles of apprehension pricking along his hairline. Liana's recent demeanor had vacillated between utter calm and sheer rage, often only minutes apart in the same conversation.

If she was this calm, any action he took could trigger a more violent response.

Well, you slept in that bed, now you have to make it right. He hit redial for the number she had used. The phone rang and rang but never kicked in to voicemail.

On the tenth ring, he hung up.

***

Liana held the phone in her hand, a smug smile crossing her lips as she spied Kirby's number lighting the screen. She counted the rings until the phone fell silent and the screen faded.

Some confrontations were better left to a face-to-face.

CHAPTER 4

Portsmouth, Virginia 1861

"Don't worry, Hank," Jack said to his friend. "Maggie's only a baby." *He smirked as he emphasized the word in a sing-song taunt. "She'll get caught first and have to be 'it' for all the rest of the games."*

"Don't call me a baby," Maggie shouted, stomping her foot.

"Baby, baby." The other kids raced circles around Maggie, chanting, "Maggie is a baby." Someone tapped her right shoulder, and when Maggie spun in that direction, no one was there. Then fingers tapped her left shoulder and she twirled in that direction, in time to catch Frank skipping behind her.

"Stop it!" Maggie pushed her brother as Hank leaned against the corner of the house and tucked his head in his arms as he began counting backwards from one hundred.

"You are such a crybaby, Maggot," Jack said, yanking her pigtail as he passed. He and his twin Frank ran in separate directions, and the rest of the cousins scattered to find hiding places in bushes and behind the carriages parked in the rear yard and alleyway.

"Ninety, eighty-nine, eighty-eight…"

So, Maggie headed to the one place the other kids refused to go, and scurried under the magnolia branches to her favorite perch. She wrinkled her nose. The earth had that funny odor, like the basement of Grandfather's house in Richmond, but mixed with the fresh smell of the green tree leaves and the coming rain.

Maggie climbed up the branches of her Aunt Celestine's big magnolia tree and settled in a crook about eight feet off the ground. The twins would never look for her here, but she tucked her skirts under her legs to be sure they couldn't see her dress. Her brothers were only eleven months older, but they used their twin strength to gang up on her whenever they could.

She leaned against the trunk and hugged her doll. Frank always claimed there were ghosts in the tree, and Jack always agreed with everything Frank said, just to go against their younger sister. They hated the low hanging branches that spread out over the ground, creating the cave-like room underneath, but she always found it a pleasant escape from the brothers, not to mention her cousins, who were siding with the twins today.

"They are all so mean." Maggie pouted and pressed her cheek to the doll's face. "All I wanted to do was play hide-and-seek with them. They said I had to be 'it' and find them."

But for once the twins had defended her, arguing that their friend Hank had to be "it" because he had been found first in the previous game, so he had covered his eyes while they scattered to hide.

"Ready or not, here I come!" Hank shouted as he ran to the alley near the tree. Maggie peeked through the leaves and could see his legs through a small opening in the foliage. She covered her mouth to prevent a giggle from escaping.

"They won't find us up here," she told her doll. Tears rolled down her cheek as she remembered the taunts from the other kids. "They are such scaredy-cats, they'll be afraid to come here, won't they, Abby?" She drew her knees up to prop the doll in her lap. Leaves rustled around her, and Maggie glanced around, frowning.

"We'll only stay here a few minutes more, Abby," she crooned to her doll. Winds whipped her bangs across her forehead.

"Oh, go away, old ghost," she muttered. "I like it here." The

breeze stopped and the leaves settled. She reached into a pocket in her pinafore and pulled out the little velvet bag she had tucked away. Smoothing the pinafore across her legs, she shook out the contents of the pouch. Mama's pretty watch and the handkerchief holding Papa's heavy emerald ring dropped in her lap. She loved Daddy's ring, with its big green stone that sparkled when he turned it in the light.

Her conscience pricked at her. She shouldn't have taken the bag.

She'd forgotten about it while she played with the kids, but holding it now, she felt bad for taking it.

The shouts from the other kids joined Hank's, calling for her to come out.

"Olly olly oxen free!" Jack called from the yard. "Come on, Maggie, we have to go inside. You are safe to come out from hiding and you won't be 'it' next time."

"Papa's gonna give you a lickin' if you don't come in," shouted Frank. He stood just outside the magnolia tree branches. Maggie stuck her tongue out, then covered her mouth to suppress another giggle when she saw his foot poking into the leaves below.

He wouldn't search further. Both of her big brothers were afraid of the dark cavern the swooping tree branches created.

"Papa might spank us for taking the bag, Abby," she whispered to her doll. She picked up the pretty gold watch, running her fingertips over the ring of tiny pearls surrounding a heart-shaped glass front. The big hand was on the twelve and the little hand almost at the three.

She counted the numbers out loud. "One-two-three. It's almost three o'clock, Abby." She held the piece to her ear and tapped the dial. Usually she could hear the ticking as the minutes passed, but it seemed the hands were frozen in position. She twisted the little knob like she had seen her mother do to wind the watch. The hands twirled backwards and then she turned the button in the opposite direction.

The wind whipped through the branches again. Some of the

leaves turned upward. Ominous rumbles rolled closer. Voices grew louder as others joined in the search, nearer ones calling from the backyard, others fading as the callers darted around the house.

"Frank, your mama said get inside right now." Hank's older sister Maisy commanded. Close by but unseen, her no-nonsense tone softened when she added, "Where are you, Maggie honey? Please show yourself. A storm is coming."

Maggie almost climbed from her perch. She liked Maisy, whose name was a Scottish version of Margaret. Maggie wished she could be called Maisy instead of the nickname she hated. Sometimes her brothers called her "Maggot" just to be really mean.

Maisy called again, her voice fading as she walked away from the tree.

A thunderclap crashed, so loud it had to be right overhead. Maggie jerked, spilling the jewelry as the bag slipped from her hands. Papa's ring hit the branch below her, separating the emerald stone from the base. Mama's watch tumbled after, hitting branch after branch. Her mouth shaped an "O" as her horrified gaze followed the jewel pieces to the ground.

Huge droplets of rain slipped through the leaves, pelting Maggie's face as she scrambled down the trunk. Her foot slipped on the last limb and she fell backwards, knocking the wind out of her lungs.

Lightning slashed outside the boughs forming the tree cave. Inside, the gnarled branches took on grotesque shapes. Maggie's fingers wrapped around the watch and she scrambled to her feet. She pushed her way through the foliage, twigs grabbing at her hair like clawing fingers, tearing Abby from her arms. Maggie tugged on the doll until it broke free. She fell on her face in the alley, landing in the path of a horse-drawn wagon.

Winds whirled debris around and around Maggie, obscuring her vision as she stood in a disoriented daze. She shielded her face with her arms, the doll in the crook of one, its clothing stinging her face as it flapped. The wind roared like a locomotive. Through the din, her mother's voice called her name. The sharp nettles of rain sliced her skin and created a curtain of water through which she could barely see. Maggie opened her mouth to answer but the downpour nearly choked her.

Disoriented, the little girl clambered toward the side of the lumbering wagon in search of cover just as a bolt of lightning pierced the sky, exploding in an eerie strobe of green-white light.

The rising scream died on her lips as an unseen hand grasped the sleeve of her dress and pulled her forward through the whirlwind.

Modern day Portsmouth, Virginia

Liana backed into a rear parking space that gave her full view of the three buildings. The café was on the far left, Clothiste's Inn in the middle, and the law office to the right. A snazzy red convertible was parked at a sign identifying the space as "Reserved for T. Dunbar." Beside the Maserati, a champagne-colored sedan parked at a sign reserved for "S. Cross."

Liana resisted the urge to take her keys and run the tips along the shiny paint jobs of both vehicles.

She cut her eyes in the direction of the bed and breakfast where Kirby's SUV was positioned. The rear door of the inn opened and Kirby stepped out first, followed by a little girl, and then Sandi. Liana shrank lower in her seat, but she had parked her car between the glare of the spotlights and doubted she could be seen. The little girl pointed upward and both adults followed her outstretched hand to gaze at the light. A flapping shape—a bat perhaps—fluttered above their heads. The child shrieked and Kirby scooped her into his arms. Sandi put her arm through the crook of his. Laughter drifted across the cold, crisp air.

Fury enveloped Liana from head to toe as she watched

trio race down the sidewalk.

"Well, aren't we just the cozy little family?" Her face distorted in contempt as she spewed the words out loud. She reached for her handbag and slipped her hand through the opening. Her fingers curled around the cold steel of her .38. Satisfaction stilled the rage.

All in due time.

Through narrowed eyes, she glared after the trio until their retreating backs disappeared in the dark. She slid from behind the wheel and walked up the rear steps of Clothiste's Inn. She peered through the window in the top half of the door. A low light burned underneath a cabinet, casting a soft beam around the spotless kitchen.

She turned the door handle. Liana could not believe her luck in finding the rear door to the inn unlocked. She entered the kitchen. Her breath formed vapors, and when she inhaled the icy air burned her throat.

"Geez, it's freaking cold in here," she said aloud. She pushed the door behind her and looked around. She walked around the island counters and poked her head in the dining room. The dimmed chandelier light cast odd shadows along the walls.

The cold air enveloped her as she wandered to the first-floor bedroom. She stepped into the small suite, and recognized a sweater she had seen Sandi wear. She picked up the navy cardigan draped over the rungs of a chair.

"So, Miss Lawyer Lady, you like to shop at the big stores, eh?" Liana said aloud as she fingered the Gucci label in the lining. "This little number easily cost a thousand bucks." She replaced the sweater, then yanked it and dropped it to the floor as she glanced around the room.

Her gaze drifted to the nightstand, where Sandi's cell phone and a pile of change sat on the lace doily. Stepping on the sweater, Liana picked up the phone and tapped the screen.

"Tsk, tsk, no password? That's not too smart, Lawyer Lady." She scrolled until she found the number to the phone. Withdrawing her own phone from her coat pocket, she slid her fingers in rapid succession across the keys, typing out the message, "Has he told you about the baby yet?" When Sandi's phone buzzed with the incoming text signal, Liana placed it back on the stand.

Then she sent a second message. "Go ahead. Ask him."

With that, Liana ground her heel into Sandi's sweater, and walked over to a small dressing table. She picked up a cosmetics bag and rummaged through the makeup kit, withdrawing a tube of lipstick. Her gaze flickered around the room, settling on the doll slumped sideways in the chair. She walked over and picked up the modern doll dressed in colonial clothes.

Pursing her lips in contempt, she removed the top from the lipstick tube. First, she applied a fresh coat on her own lips, so practiced that she did not need a mirror to complete a perfect application. Then she angled the tip of the lipstick to color the doll's lips in a little red bow shape. Turning her head from side to side, she studied the vinyl face before swiping a single line from each corner of the mouth to an ear. She propped the toy in a sitting position.

Crossing the room toward the door, Liana tossed the lipstick on the bed. She crushed her boot into Sandi's sweater one more time, then headed out the door and paused in the hallway. She turned out the light and stepped into the hallway.

Turning left down the short corridor, she walked up the stairwell leading to the guest bedrooms of the inn. On each door, a brass plaque proclaimed the name of the room. One bore "The Antebellum" another "The Victorian." She peeked inside each one. Decorated in the period identified on their plaques, both appeared unoccupied.

She moved to the closed door marked "The Colonial." She and Kirby would have spent a weekend in this suite had he not walked in on her with Spencer.

She hadn't been particularly enthused about the stay— or about being with Kirby any longer, for that matter. It was his fault she had turned to Spencer. Sure, Kirby was injured in Afghanistan helping people, but his leg was so mangled, he wasn't perfect in her eyes anymore.

You had such a beautiful body, Kirby, until you got hurt. It's all your fault I turned away from you.

Justification easing her guilt, Liana tried the knob and the ornate handle opened. She peeked inside. A shirt she had once given Kirby was draped across the back of a high-backed chair. She fingered the collar. *Ah! He still loves me. He still wears the things I bought for him.* Every sign indicated he slept in the room alone and his lawyer lady slept downstairs.

So maybe he wasn't sleeping with her after all.

She'd had every intention of trashing his room but tamped down the urge. *Maybe I have a chance to win you back, Kirby.* Her mind conflicted with itself. *Even if you are not perfect anymore.* She left the room as she found it and walked the few steps to the top of the stairs.

She looked down. A few steps down led to a small landing, and with a left turn, the last steps led to the foyer.

Liana stepped on the first tread. A fresh blast of cold hit her in the face and she shivered. Kirby had told her that someone in his family had been pushed down these very steps in colonial days. Even before she knew that, she'd never understood his fascination with the inn, so cozily tucked between the French café on one side and the law office of his bitch lawyer lady and her even bitchier law partner on the other.

She walked down the last of the stairs. Another wave of cold sent her into shivers as she strode toward the parlor. The room, tastefully decorated in colonial style, sported a sofa on one wall and two wingback chairs on opposite sides of the fireplace. End tables held knickknacks and tourist brochures.

As she walked further inside, the room flashed in light. For a second the parlor was decorated with different furniture, similar to the antebellum setting she had once seen through the window.

Liana cringed and shook her head, then opened her eyes to look around her. The colonial furniture surrounded her, and the room appeared normal.

Until she noticed the frosty streaks covering the mirror above the mantel. She moved closer, and ran her finger across the rime, leaving a momentary clear band that immediately clouded again.

She eyed the heavy silver candlesticks on opposite ends. She used one finger to push the candlestick on her left back and forth before moving down the length of the fireplace shelf.

How stupid to leave such valuables in a place where anyone could just walk away with them. Liana trailed her fingers over the clock, then reached for the other candlestick. She gripped the base and gasped in pain. The heat seared her skin, leaving a red mark on her palm.

The overhead lights flickered and Liana shivered.

"Thinking of stealing again, darlin'?" a male voice drawled in her ear.

Cold breath swept across her skin. Liana whirled on one foot. Her eyes widened in panic at the man standing before her. She clutched her chest. "Peter! Where did you come from? How did you get in here?"

"That's a long story. Doors open and close all the time. You just have to wait for the opportunity to enter. And here I am." He shrugged, palms up, then crossed his arms over his barrel chest, feet planted wide apart. "How the hell are you, Liana? That is the name you call yourself now, isn't it?

"I'm not going back with you, Peter." Even as she emphasized the words in a firm tone, Liana edged close to a wing chair to put distance between her and Peter.

"Oh, you're coming with me, all right, darlin'." Peter took two steps toward her. "I was arrested because of you, you bitch, for a crime I didn't commit."

"I didn't know that, Peter, honest I didn't."

"Honest? You? Don't make me laugh. How could you not know I went to prison? You let me take the blame for a grand larceny—a felony. But then again, you never even acknowledged what you had done. You never even contacted me. It was like you just disappeared off the face of the earth."

"I-I wasn't there, Peter. I left—I left town before the trial. I knew they would blame you, but I made a new life for myself. If I'd confessed, they would have sent me to prison. I could never have survived if they sent me there. It's easier for a man…"

"Don't even try that. I damn near lost everything because of you." His glance angled toward the clock before he turned a hard, steely gaze on Liana. "You've been nothing but a selfish, take-all bitch your whole life, and it's time you paid for your deeds. I'm not letting you out of my sight until we get this squared away."

"No, Peter," Liana shouted as Peter grabbed for her arms. "I'm not going back with you." She wrenched her wrist free from his grasp and stumbled backward backwards over the ottoman, knocking her purse over and spilling the contents.

The .38 clattered to the floor. Liana dove for the weapon but Peter was faster. He stomped on the barrel, then kicked her hand away, eyeing the gun with anger.

"Now just what were you planning to do with that, darlin'?" Peter's drawl mocked her. With the toe of his heavy leather boot, he pushed the gun under one of the matching wing chairs.

Liana rolled to a sitting position and pressed her injured hand to her chest, glaring in silence. Her driver's license had fallen to the floor and he picked it up.

"Nice picture. I see you shaved quite a few years off your age." Voice laced with sarcasm, he tossed the card aside and wrenched Liana to her feet, clutching her upper arms in a firm grip. He spun her until her back was to his chest. He wrapped one hand around her neck, pressing until she gurgled.

"I'd kill you right here, but you're not worth going back to jail for. However, let me make this clear. If you don't come back with me and make this right, I will kill you."

No one would hear her if she screamed, but he moved his hand up her throat and clapped his palm over her mouth. With the other, he clamped her against his chest in a vise-like grip. Liana struggled to escape but she was no match for him as he dragged her with him.

CHAPTER 5

Clearing a space on the table, Stephanie flopped a pad of paper open and poised her pen over the page. "While we are waiting for Beth and Connor to arrive with Tanner, we can update Kirby and Sandi. You may remember that we found hundreds of old letters in several different locations from various descendants of Étienne and Clothiste, passed down for generations in old trunks and cases, and in no particular order. Kyle and I went over more notes in the family papers, but we didn't find anything of relevance yet."

Kyle peered over her shoulder. "Stephanie and Mary Jo had their ghostly visitors. We know Kirby and Terry each had significant paranormal events happen to them in the parlor of Clothiste's Inn around midnight. Then Sandi and Norrie were caught up in the tail end of Kirby's entry into the—I don't know what to call it other than time warp—at midnight. Then they arrived back around three p.m. with just a few hours lost in their real time, but with Maggie instead of Norrie. We expect there will be a specific moment in time that will return the two little girls to their rightful places, but we don't know when, we can only guess based on the past events."

With a nod, Stephanie continued. "We discovered that

a significant storm struck the area on the day Maggie disappeared in eighteen sixty-one. Stephanie uncovered her missing teardrop jewel and Nicole's doll during Hurricane Abby. Bad weather was present at various times during Terry's and Kirby's respective incidents."

"I used to dream often of storms," Mary Jo interjected. "Does that count?"

Kyle shrugged. "We honestly have no idea, Mary Jo, so, we are going out on a limb here. I'm suggesting that because we expect bad weather over the next few hours, and storms are so often associated with the paranormal activities, we may have the potential for something to happen tonight." Kyle glanced over Stephanie's neatly organized notes.

"Why do you say that, Kyle?" Chase asked. He placed his arm on the back of Mary Jo's chair in a protective manner. She smiled, and in a rare form of public affection, the stoic former soldier kissed her fiancé.

"Well, several unscientific reasons. Stormy weather. The four colonial children each had jewels that were passed down to descendants into the possessions of this most current generation, all of whom are present here today. While Norrie is not a descendant of the family, she has in her custody the nineteenth century doll of a child—Margaret—who *was* a descendant of Louis and who now has in her possession Norrie's twenty-first century doll. All of the conditions may be in place for a possible paranormal event."

Gage leaned forward on the table, a frown creasing his usually-relaxed face. "I don't think I like the sound of this."

Stephanie gave his hand a reassuring pat, but his scowl deepened. "Gage, we are in uncharted waters here. None of us are paranormal experts, and there isn't anyone who could help, even if they believed our story."

"Ghostbusters?" Chase mumbled, breaking the tension.

"Good one, Chase, we needed that. I have my necklace." Stephanie pointed to her teardrop diamond pendant. She glanced around, nodded when Mary Jo displayed the ruby heart. Terry used a finger around her collar to lift the chain holding the cross with the sapphire. All eyes turned in Kirby's direction. He slumped in the chair, hands in his pockets, and his shoulders hunched. He stared toward the wall, a faraway look in his eyes.

"Kirby, do you have your ring?" Stephanie asked.

No answer.

"Earth to Kirby?" Gage snapped his fingers near Kirby's ear.

"What?" Kirby shook his head, his eyes coming to focus as he glanced around the table. With a sheepish smile, he said, "I'm sorry, I was on a side trip. I'm back now. What did you say?"

"You've been drifting all evening, cousin." Gage formed a fist and lightly tapped his relative's shoulder.

"Sorry," Kirby said again, shoving the text message from his thoughts. He would tell Sandi everything tonight.

Kyle repeated the comments he and Stephanie had presented, and when he asked about the ring, Kirby raised his hand with the knuckles outward to show the emerald.

"What do we do now, sit and wait? For what?" Gage asked as he rose from the table. "Suppose someone else gets caught in this time travel? There can't be many portals for this phenomenon to happen, otherwise people would come and go all the time. Maggie has been gone for over one hundred and fifty years, you know."

"Shh," Stephanie lowered her voice in warning.

Maggie, who had been coloring quietly at a table in the corner looked up. "Am I in trouble?" she asked, hand poised with crayon in mid-air.

"Not at all, sweetie," Sandi assured her. She crossed over to the child and sat in the chair next to her. "We are just trying to figure out how to get you home. You see, we think we might be able to take you back to your mama and papa soon. We just don't know how yet."

Maggie opened her mouth to speak but was interrupted by the boisterous voice of Tanner as he stomped up the steps outside. The front door of the café burst open and he bolted through the door, sending the brass bell overhead into a frenzy of ringing.

"Hey, you guys!" He shouted as he thundered toward the tables! "It's snowing outside!"

"Snowing?" Maggie scooted from the table, tipping the tray that held her crayons. She pressed her nose to the glass of the bay window.

"Calm down, Tanner," Connor said. "It's only a few icy pellets spattering down."

Tanner didn't answer, his attention on the little girl he had never seen before. "Who are you?" he asked, tilting his head to the left as he studied her.

"I'm Margaret," she answered, stepping back to Sandi and clutching her hand. "But my brothers call me Maggie. I like Margaret better."

Tanner closed the distance between him and his cousin from the past, eying her solemnly. "Your brothers said to come home, they miss you."

The room fell silent as eyes turned toward the clairvoyant boy.

"What did you say, honey?" Beth asked gently, dropping to her knees beside him, and taking his hand. Her pregnant state was more evident as her coat slipped open and she plopped into a sitting position.

"The twins said they want her to come home." Tanner took his psychic powers in stride and seemed unaffected by voices from the past speaking to him. He picked up a crayon in one mitten-covered hand and began coloring on a loose paper while still allowing his mother to grip his left hand.

"Honey, can you talk to me for a minute?" Beth prodded. She removed his left mitten, and reached for his right. He held his hand out so she could remove the mitten and then shrugged out of his coat before returning to his coloring of SpongeBob SquarePants. "We are trying to help Maggie—Margaret—get home to her family, and maybe you can help. Are those boys here in the room with us now?" She glanced around.

Tanner gave an eye roll skyward. "Oh, Mo-om. No—they aren't ghosts. But I can hear them in my head."

Beth placed her hand over her heart and turned imploring eyes toward Connor, who held his arms out to his son.

"Come here, buddy. We just need to ask you some questions to help everyone out. When you get finished, we will take you to McDonald's if you want to go."

Beth mirrored her son's eyeroll but said nothing as her husband scooped Tanner into his arms. She lumbered to her feet.

"Can she come too?" Tanner pointed to Maggie.

"Probably not, son." Connor hefted his son to a more comfortable position and tilted the boy's chin until they made eye contact. "We have to leave before the weather gets worse, and the most important thing is to get Maggie home. Can you hear anything else? Are the twins talking to you?"

Tanner sloped his head as if listening and shrugged.

"Nope. That's all they said. 'Tell Maggie to come home. We miss her.'"

"They were mean to me," Maggie pouted, then a tear rolled down her cheek. "But I miss them too."

"Don't be sad." Tanner wriggled from his father's grasp. "You'll get home. Here, you can have my mittens to take with you."

"NO!" Stephanie and Beth shouted together. The two children turned to them with wide eyes.

"We'll find something else for Maggie, okay, sweetie?" Beth added.

"What are these yellow things?" Maggie tapped the hand coverings Beth had piled on the table, pointing as she stared intently at strange yellow figures on the fronts.

"Those are Minions. Haven't you ever seen them?" Tanner looked at Maggie as if she must have come from Mars.

Maggie shook her head. Tanner picked up one navy blue mitten and pointed to a goggle-wearing face. "This one is Stuart. See? He has one eye. And the other one is Mike. He has two eyes in his goggles."

Maggie stared harder, then looked at Tanner. Suddenly a giggle burst forth, erupting into a snicker. Tanner joined in. Within seconds, the two children rolled in helpless laughter, their beguiling mirth bringing smiles to the adults' faces.

After they calmed down, Tanner asked, "Can I show Maggie the miniature cooking stuff in *Le Petite Chef*?" Her referred to Mary Jo's pint-sized kitchen in a separate room where she conducted cooking classes for kids.

Tanner hopped from foot to foot as he waited. "And then can I get my toy bucket to play with?"

Beth often helped out in the café during the lunch hour and brought Tanner with her on the days Connor was on duty. The bucket was filled to the brim with toys to keep the boy occupied while she worked.

"Yes, but then you come right back here and sit where I can see you."

"Yes, ma'am. Come on, Margaret." Tanner in the lead, the two children dashed toward the little kitchen.

"I don't want anything of Tanner's going back in time," Beth warned, clenching her jaw firmly.

"Don't worry, babe, we'll do a complete inventory of him before we leave," Connor said. He scratched his neck where the collar stuck up, then shrugged out of his coat. "What do you make of all that talk from Maggie?"

Kyle raised his hands palms up. "Beats me. But she did—does—did have twin brothers, so we have to assume he's getting messages from them."

"This gives me the creeps." Beth shivered.

Mary Jo carried a tray of steaming mugs to the table. "Have some tea, Beth." As if she anticipated Beth's next questions, she added, "It's decaffeinated."

"Got anything stronger?" Chase asked.

"Sorry. You know I don't have a liquor license." She offered tea or hot chocolate, and when the tray was empty of mugs, went to the kitchen for more.

While childish giggles emerged from the direction of *Le Petite Chef*, the adults engaged in idle chitchat, no one able to offer an explanation or a solution to the dilemma they faced.

An odd rumble of thunder rattled the windows, startling the gathering. "Geez, can it get any stranger than that?" Chase asked.

Maggie screamed and ran back into the dining area, straight into Sandi's arms. Tanner followed, silent but with eyes wide. He stood to the side, arms full of action figures and toys.

"What is it, Tanner Bear?" Terry asked, using the family nickname. She held her hand up slightly and shook her head when Beth moved. The other adults remained silent, their concerned stares directed at the boy.

"She has to go home tonight," he said, worry lining his little face.

"Why do you say that?"

"I don't know why, Aunt Terry. I just know it." He turned to Stephanie and a tear trailed down his face. "Nickel says to bring her teardrop."

"What?" Stephanie clapped her hands to her mouth in shock. Nickel was Tanner's interpretation of the name Nicole. Shortly after Stephanie had arrived in Portsmouth, she had encountered the image of a child surrounded by shimmering blue light. The apparition had never spoken to her, but somehow communicated messages to Tanner which he then relayed to Stephanie, in much the same manner as he had just done.

"I thought you didn't see Nicole anymore," Terry prompted gently.

"I didn't see her. I heard her voice, after the twins said Margaret had to come home. Nicole told me to tell Stephanie to bring her teardrop." Tanner dropped his armload of toys on the table, his bottom lip trembling. "I'm sad now. Why can't I see Nickel anymore? Even Grandma Nickel doesn't come to see me anymore."

Despite her gentle questions, Terry could not get any further information from either child. "It's coming up on nine o'clock," she said, looking around the room. "Why don't we clean this place up as quick as possible and go back to the inn?"

Sandi jumped to her feet to clear the table, but Mary Jo shook her head. "We've got this. There are enough of us here to get this done in five minutes. You and Kirby take Maggie back, calm her down."

"And, please, Sandi," Beth implored. "Make sure that she doesn't have anything of Tanner's with her that could—you know—cause problems later."

"We will, Beth," Sandi said. Kirby retrieved their jackets from the coatrack. First, they bundled Maggie in Norrie's blue Dora the Explorer coat, then shrugged into their own. By the time they were ready to say goodbyes, the dining area of the café was nearly cleaned."

Sandi hugged both of Tanner's parents before grabbing the little boy in a tight embrace. "Tell Norrie I love her, if you can," she whispered in his ear, choking past the lump in her throat.

"She knows," he whispered back.

Thunder rolled again as Kirby, Sandi, and Maggie dashed through the rain to return to Clothiste's Inn.

***

Only a few miles away, raindrops smacked against the windows of buildings in the Naval Regional Medical Center Portsmouth, originally known as the Portsmouth Naval Hospital. Medical staff and patients in the modern buildings paid no mind to the inclement weather as they went on with routine life.

Not far away, the venerable older buildings, some built even before the facility admitted its first patients in 1830, shook with another heavy boom of thunder.

In a darkened office of the historic old Building 1, however, lights flashed on and off, illuminating a room under renovation. One section of wall was stripped to the studs. Lined with new insulation and ready for workers to soon sheetrock and plaster, the walls appeared skeletal in the eerie flashing of the lights.

A third thunderclap, more ominous and percussive, rattled the glass in the window. Two studs, separated by a mere centimeter, joined together to create the window frame. A minuscule corner of a piece of paper, wedged between the wall stud and the one that made up the window frame, peeked out between the wooden supports.

Darkness followed each flash of the malfunctioning lights.

After the fifth flash, the lights remained off.

But the tiny sliver of paper grew larger, as if pushed by unseen hands, until a full envelope emerged. Now free of its hiding place, the envelope fluttered to the floor and landed face-down.

***

"Uh-oh." Kirby paused at the kitchen door, hand over the lock. He glanced at Sandi as the door opened inward at his touch.

Kirby stepped into the kitchen and flicked the light switch. "Stay here with Margaret," he whispered.

"Take this." Sandi pressed her gun in his hand. He raised an eyebrow and she shrugged. She picked the little girl up and held her tight.

Kirby made a quick sweep around the first floor, then poked his head around the kitchen door. "I'm going to check the bedrooms upstairs." He left, and returned five minutes later.

"No sign of anyone. Maybe the wind just blew it open."

"That lock keeps messing up. I know Terry had it on her to-do list of repairs for Chase," Sandi said, relief evident in her voice. She lowered Margaret to the floor, and Kirby gave her back the gun. She slipped it back into her purse and the trio headed toward the parlor.

"May I get my doll from our room, please?" Margaret asked.

Sandi nodded and the little girl skipped away to the innkeeper's suite. "Considering all she has been through, that is the politest child I have ever met," she said to Kirby.

"Oh, I don't know about that." Kirby moved forward and circled his arms around Sandi's waist. "From what I've seen, Norrie has some pretty good manners."

"I try…" A piercing scream interrupted Sandi and the two adults looked at each other before scrambling toward the suite.

"We're coming, Margaret," Kirby called.

Margaret stood frigid, holding her doll at arm's length, shaking.

Sandi bounded to her side. "What is it, honey?"

She froze when she noticed the grotesque markings on the doll's face and said over her shoulder, "Kirby, someone has been in here. Look at the doll." She took the marred figure and handed it to Kirby, then gathered the little girl in a hug.

Glancing around the room, Sandi's gaze dropped to the sweater scrunched on the floor. She pointed. "Look at my sweater. Let's leave everything as it is and we'll call the police."

Kirby reached for Margaret. She wrapped her arms tight around his neck and buried her face in his shoulder as he led the way from the room.

Following behind, Sandi reached for her cellphone, ignoring the message indicating she had missed texts, and dialed 911. After explaining the nature of her call, she hung up and tapped numbers again. Terry's voicemail kicked in.

"Hey, Terry, it's Sandi. I think there was a break-in at the inn. We're waiting on the police. Call me when you get this message."

She slipped the phone into her pocket and frowned, tilting her head to one side as she studied the living room. "I don't see anything missing in here, but things are out of place. Those candlesticks are not where they usually are, and this ottoman is out of place." She stepped further into the room, Margaret clinging to her side.

"And...oh, shit." Sandi pointed to the spilled contents of the purse scattered on the floor between the footstool and the chair.

Kirby leaned over and glanced at the driver's license face up on the floor. "Liana's been here." His gaze swept the area and landed on the .38 that had been kicked under the chair.

Margaret screamed again. She broke free from Sandi and dropped to her knees beside the stool. A dull gold but ornate timepiece had slipped out of its tissue wrapping. Margaret pointed with a trembling finger.

"Mama's watch, Mama's watch!" Before Sandi could stop her, the child had pulled a brooch watch from the mix of cosmetics, wallet, and other contents.

A bolt of lightning flashed and thunder crashed outside. The interior lights flickered. The candlesticks rattled on the mantle. A magazine on the coffee table flipped open, its pages fluttering as if turned by unseen hands.

Then the room grew quiet. Kirby knelt in front of Margaret. "Margaret, honey, why do you think this is your mama's watch?"

"It is, it is." The youngster sucked in air as she sobbed. "I took Mama's reticule with her watch and Papa's ring and hid in the tree to play with them. I dropped them and the storm came. I ran from under the tree and a man grabbed me in the horse and wagon. There was a lady, too. And thunder boomed and made me cover my ears." The moment she said the word thunder, the darkness outside the bay window lit up with another jagged blue streak, immediately followed by a rumbling clap.

Margaret covered ears with her hands and screamed again.

The mirror over the mantle shuddered against the wall. Wavy motions took over the smooth surface of quicksilver while weak green and iridescent lights glinted in the background.

Somewhere in Time

The infinite twisting and twirling through the dark passageway came to an abrupt end when Peter's burly shoulder crashed against a solid wall. He maintained a grip on Liana's wrist, digging his fingers into her skin to ensure she could not break away.

She shook her hand, trying to pull away from him but her body dragged with unimaginable weight.

"Let me go," she cried.

"You aren't getting away, CarlyAnna," Peter warned as he tightened his hold. "Oh, excuse me, I meant Liana."

A tiny square of light appeared in the gloom, moving out of reach as he slapped the walls. He followed the diminishing light as he moved around, dragging Liana with him. He banged the walls, turning sharp corners, and continuing until he had repeated the movements in a square. He slapped the solid partition, then dragged Liana through the maneuvers again, turning corner and moving to the next wall, ignoring her cry when she bumped into the wall.

"Where are we?" she asked. She reached out with her free hand and brushed against the barrier.

Just enough stingy light from the opening illuminated his face as

65

he looked at Liana.

"Looks like we're lost somewhere in time, CarlyAnna darlin'," he drawled. "Somewhere I've been trapped for more than a hundred and fifty years."

The square of miserly light shrunk to a tiny dot and disappeared, plunging the couple into pitch black.

Kirby took Sandi's hand. "Something is trying to happen, but it's not strong enough. We need to get the others here. I'll try to call Terry again."

Commotion at the back door interrupted him.

As quickly as it started, the phenomena ended. The room returned to normal.

Footsteps and the staticky squelch of a police radio preceded the arrival of Terry leading a uniformed officer into the parlor.

"What's going on?" she asked. "We just ran into Officer Philbin coming up the steps and he said he was responding to a possible burglary here."

Sandi recognized Officer John Philbin from cases in court proceedings and greeted him as they shook hands.

Then she asked, "Terry, are Stephanie and Mary Jo with you?"

"They're waiting outside. The dispatcher explained that you were inside. John needs to see the scene before any more people come in." Terry introduced the patrolman to Kirby.

The men shook hands. Kirby said, "I'm afraid we moved things a bit. We didn't realize there had been a break-in right away. We found the door open and I made a quick visual check. Everything seemed okay. Then Margaret found lipstick markings on her doll and we realized someone had actually been inside. We've searched all the rooms. Only this room and the innkeeper's suite seemed to have been disturbed." He turned to the child curled in a ball asleep on the couch. Sandi slipped an afghan over Margaret's huddled form.

"John, may I wash the doll's face so that I can give it to Margaret? The clothes cover the body, so I doubt there are fingerprints." Sandi took the doll from Kirby. "She will want it when she wakes up. My lipstick tube may have Liana's fingerprints on it."

"Let me take some photos first."

After the officer photographed the doll, Sandi soaped away the lipstick markings and brought the figure to the couch. She tucked it under Margaret's arm.

"Is it okay for me to step outside with the others, John?" she asked, buttoning her jacket.

The patrolman nodded as he removed a notepad from his jacket pocket. "Please don't touch anything."

As Kirby's calm voice relayed the story to the officer, Sandi motioned for Terry to follow. Under the small overhang covering the back porch, Gage and Stephanie, Mary Jo and Chase, and Kyle clustered to avoid the cold rain dripping from the gutters.

"What happened?" Stephanie asked.

Sandi shook her head. "We don't know exactly. When we got back here, Kirby went to unlock the door and it pushed open. I know it doesn't always latch but I forgot to check behind us when we went to the café." She explained what they discovered, including the gun and the spilled contents of Liana's purse.

"Who is Liana?" Chase asked.

"Kirby's ex-girlfriend. They broke up recently."

Sandi then described Margaret's response to seeing the antique timepiece. The odd event led to a barrage of questions from her friends. Then she held up her hands.

"Listen, you guys. There's something else. A really

strange thing happened, like an—I don't know how to describe it except maybe other-world occurrence. After the thunder and lightning…"

"There wasn't any thunder or lightning after you left," Terry interrupted.

"What are you talking about? The inn practically rattled right off its foundation."

"No." Terry shook her head. "We didn't hear a thing and we were right next door."

"Nothing except those couple of rumbles when you were there," Stephanie said. The others nodded in agreement.

Sandi held a hand up. "We had several blinding flashes light up the windows, followed by rumbles of thunder." She described the eerie happenings, concluding with, "Kirby thinks something was about to happen, but the setting just too weak. We think whatever is coming will transpire tonight once all of you are together. I hope Kirby doesn't mention that part to the officer, we'll sound like raving lunatics."

The group broke into another babble of questions, interrupted only when Gage and Chase returned. The latter said, "Everything seems okay around the buildings. All of our vehicles are okay, but we noticed a strange car in the parking lot. Dark-colored BMW."

"It might be Liana's. I don't know her car." Sandi shrugged and pulled her coat tighter.

"We can let the police know it's there and they can check it out."

At that moment, Kirby poked his head outside the door and said, "You guys can come back inside now and get warm. The officer's lifted some fingerprints but needs someone to tell him if anything is missing." He went back inside.

"I'll check. Kyle, will you come with me?" Terry led the others in a single file. Once inside the warmth of the kitchen, she and Kyle followed Kirby around the counter to the parlor, where Officer Philbin stood as he jotted on a clipboard. The rest remained in the kitchen and gathered around the butcher-block island.

Sandi drew her cellphone from her pocket and checked her text messages. She didn't recognize one number and scrolled to the message.

Has he told you about the baby yet?

She held the phone askance.

"What is it, Sandi?" Stephanie walked to her side.

"Nothing, really. Wrong number texted me, I guess." Sandi scrolled to the next message.

Go ahead. Ask him.

She pushed the callback number.

A shrill peal from the direction of the living room matched time with the ringing in her phone. She walked to the doorway separating the dining room from the parlor. Kirby, Terry, and Officer Philbin eyed Liana's phone as the screen lit up and the device vibrated on the coffee table alongside the contents of her purse.

Sandi tapped the red icon and the ringtone stopped— on her phone as well as the one on the coffee table.

"That was me calling. I had a missed call, apparently from that phone. I didn't know it was Liana's." She fought to keep her voice steady although blood rushed to her head, pulsing in her ears to match the thunder in her heart. She avoided Kirby's eyes, and when he walked toward her, she stiffened and shook her head.

"Chase and Gage said that there is a dark BMW in the parking lot, in the unlit part between the lights." Her calm, clear voice belied the turmoil churning through her.

Kirby nodded. "Liana drives a dark blue BMW."

"Do you need to ask me anything else, John?" Sandi asked.

"No." Philbin glanced at his clipboard. "I have Commander Lawrence's report and your contact info. I've taken photographs, dusted for prints, and will secure Ms. Chambers' property. She may have been startled by your return and dropped her bag in her haste to get away. She could have slipped out the front door before you got inside." He made a few more notes on his clipboard, then followed Terry out to the kitchen.

Sandi dropped onto the couch beside Margaret's sleeping form. She settled the cover over the child's shoulders and hunched into the cushions. Kirby made a move to sit on the arm of the couch, but she blocked it with her arm.

"What's wrong?" he asked.

Sandi pulled her phone out and scrolled to the message from Liana. Without glancing at Kirby, she turned her wrist, holding the phone up to show him the screen.

"Sandi, I-I…"

"Don't say a word," she whispered hoarsely. She glanced over her shoulder. No one else had entered the room. "I may need you for whatever happens tonight, but I want you out of my life. I don't want you near me or my daughter."

"Sandi, let me explain…"

With a shake of her head, Sandi stiffened her arm and held her hand palm out. "Did you know?"

Kirby paused, then nodded. "I found a message from her when we first returned, but…"

Sandi kept her gaze averted. "I have nothing to say right now, Kirby. I want my daughter home and that is all I'm going to think about or discuss. Now leave me alone." She dropped to the couch, and leaned forward, elbows on knees as she pressed her fingertips to her temples.

Kirby walked to the fireplace, back stiff with tension. He crossed his arms, staring at the floor.

Stephanie entered the parlor carrying a small box. "We've got the inevitable pot of coffee brewing," she began.

She stopped short as she took in the edgy scene in front of her.

Gage, who was following just behind her, bumped into her. "What's the matter?"

Terry and Kyle joined them next. Kirby kept his gaze on the floor. Sandi picked invisible lint from the throw covering Margaret. Neither answered.

Terry looked first at the tense couple, then to Stephanie, who lifted her shoulders in puzzlement.

Terry then asked, "Is something wrong?"

"No, nothing's wrong," Sandi snapped. "Everything is. I want this hocus-pocus bullshit to end and I want my baby home safe and sound."

"We're going to do everything we can to bring her back," Terry said.

"We'll all help in whatever way we can, Sandi," Stephanie added. "We have everything here that connects us to the past, as well as the doll that belongs to Norrie— and I have this." She opened the box and withdrew an old toy doll. "This is the doll I found in the attic after Hurricane Abby. It once belonged to Nicole and was left behind. I don't know if it has significance to any events that may happen tonight. It just seemed like a good idea to bring it along." She sat in one of the twin wing chairs and Gage sank to the floor at her feet.

"It can't hurt," Mary Jo said as she carried a tray laden

with mugs. Chase followed with a pot of coffee, which he set on a trivet on the coffee table. Mary Jo plopped into one of the wing chairs, and Chase dropped to the floor by her knees, stretching his long legs out as he mirrored Gage's position.

No one spoke. Lack of conversation in the room turned deafening, the only sound that of the mantle clock tick-tocking its way toward midnight. When the hands clicked to the 11:45 position, the clock emitted the single quarter-hour clang.

Standing just inches from the antique timepiece, Kirby started at the unexpected noise. He sat on the hearth. "I wonder, if there is more time travel will I go back to the same point in time and relive what I have had already experienced?"

The room remained silent for more several minutes until Kyle spoke. He held his hands palm up and shrugged. "We just have no way of knowing what will happen or who will go, Kirby. This is all unknown territory. Maybe if I'd been a physicist instead of a history prof, I could at least hypothesize. But I doubt if even my esteemed colleagues in that field could answer your question, although they would surely think me crazy if I asked. Theoretically it is impossible to travel back in time, but obviously it can happen, as you and Sandi have experienced. Margaret also did, because she somehow went back in time from her century to the seventeenth. There is a kind of anomaly at work here that has something to do with the weather and the objects in this room." He nodded toward the fireplace, with the mirror hanging above and the antique clock and candlesticks adorning the mantle. "Except for the worry about the two girls returning to their rightful times, I would love to be in on this experience."

"How is this going to affect the rest of us in this room?" Gage queried. "I don't want Stephanie going back in time. Or forward, or whatever. Or for that matter, I don't want Terry to go. Why can't I be the one to go? I am a descendant of Theresé, too."

Kyle scratched his head, ruffling his hair into spikes. "Well, the spirits of your ancestors have only appeared to Stephanie, Mary Jo, Terry, and Kirby, right?"

Gage nodded reluctantly. Then he said, "I saw Nicole once."

"And Marie Josephé appeared to me once," Chase offered as he bit back a yawn.

"Only because you two skeptics didn't really believe what we saw." Mary Jo nudged Chase, who answered with another yawn.

"But that doesn't mean I can't be the one to go," Gage argued.

"Mary Jo's right, sweetie, I don't think your visitation counts," Stephanie said. "And you're not in possession of one of the jewels. We thought we had already settled with all of the ghosts because no one has seen any of the girl ghosts for a while. Things were so quiet after we identified whose skeleton was buried under the old magnolia and then we reburied the bones in a proper grave. But—there must be something that still has to be finished and somehow, it affects those of us with the old family jewels in our possession. That's my unscientific theory."

"Well, I plan on going with you if anything happens." Gage reached up for Stephanie's hand and drew her out of the wingchair to the floor beside him. With his back against the front, he settled her beside him and wrapped his arms around her. She smiled and leaned her cheek against his chest.

Margaret suddenly stirred and sat bolt upright on the couch, her eyes frozen in a sleepwalker's stare as she clutched the doll to her chest.

"Is it time yet?" she asked before dropping back on her side, fast asleep. Her upturned hand slipped out from under the cover. As her fingers relaxed, the heavy gold timepiece dangled from her fingers.

"Oh, shoot, I forgot all about that." Sandi sucked in a breath. She tried to draw the watch away, but Margaret stirred again and clasped her fingers tighter around the timepiece.

Sandi explained how the little girl had reacted upon spotting the watch among the contents spilled from Liana's purse.

"The glass is cracked and scratched. It doesn't work and the hands were stuck at three o'clock. I didn't even notice she still had it when the officer gathered Liana's belongings to take into evidence. And just now, I saw the watch face again. Did any of you see that the time before Margaret clutched it in her hand?"

She glanced around at each of her friends, who shook their heads in turn. "The hands haven't moved from the three o'clock position."

Her gaze flickered to the clock on the mantle, ticking away the minutes.

"I'm convinced three will be the magic hour."

CHAPTER 6

Portsmouth, Virginia 1861

After she had taken the jewels, the thieving maid snuck into a storage building and remained there all night, scrunched in a cob-web-covered corner between garden tools and watering cans. Only a single street separated her from the Wyatt house where she'd worked. If the theft went undiscovered until morning, she might have a chance to get away.

Mosquitoes feasted on her in the sultry night, while unseen creatures skittered and squeaked inches away. As the sun rose, small slivers of daylight shined through cracks in the walls. Throughout the long day the temperature rose to an oppressive heat. Her fingers often caressed the jewelry pieces in her small bag, bringing her a measure of comfort throughout her misery. Sweat trickled down her back and pooled under her armpits, but she remained in her cramped quarters.

Where was he? *He'd promised he would come for her in the wagon as soon as he finished work. He should have returned to the shed by now. His carriage had rumbled back and forth several time as he worked. He should be finished by now.*

All she wanted was to get to Richmond and he was her only hope. He'd been furious when she came to his back door. He wouldn't have even helped her at all, except for the lies she told.

He said she'd have to wait in the shed until the next day, when he would take her at three o'clock.

Vowing this would be her last moment of poverty and servitude, she leaned her head against the wall and dozed.

A clap of thunder roused her from the fitful nap. Voices shouted outside and a thud resonated through the wooden walls as someone pushed against the door. The creaking portal swung open, sending a blinding beam of daylight into the shack. A shadowy figure silhouetted in the doorway. She clutched the bag close and shrank as far into the corner as she could.

"Maggot, are you in here?" a youthful voice shouted. "Mama says you best quit hiding and get into the house before the storm hits." Another boy's voice encouraged him to look further inside.

"I ain't going in, Frank. You go."

"Naw, I ain't going in either. Besides, Maggie's too scared to hide in a place like this, Jack." Thunder rolled in the distance.

Frank called into the glom again. "If you're hiding in here, Maggie, you're gonna be in trouble. I hope you get bit by a mouse." He slammed the door shut and slid the wooden bar in place.

The maid froze. Less light crept into the shed as the bolt held the door tight.

"Did you see anything in there, boys?" A girl's voice shouted right outside the corner of the building.

The maid cowered lower.

"No, Maisy!" The boys called in unison, their footsteps thumping as they ran by.

"Well, keep looking everywhere," the girl said. "We need to find her before the storm hits." Thunder grew louder as their voices faded.

"Oh, no. No!" The maid scrambled to her knees, knocking over a rake and a hoe as she crawled to the entrance and shoved her shoulder against the door.

The plank held fast, trapping her in the sweltering shadows.

Moments later, the door opened, and she nearly fell into the burly arms of her rescuer.

Peter!

"What took you so long to get here?" She hissed the words through her teeth as she scrambled from the oppressive shed and into a waiting wagon. The man at the reins did not answer, nor did he offer his hand. She settled in the seat behind him. He clicked his tongue and pulled the reins to move the horses. The lurching movement threw her against hi shoulder and he shrugged her away.

Gusts of wind blew debris and leaves along the narrow path. The wagon listed as the wheels rolled through the along the ruts.

"Why are you going down this road?" She hunched in the seat when he turned down the alley that ran behind the Wyatt house.

"The other lane is blocked at one end, so we have to go this way." The driver turned and looked at her. *"What else have you done?"*

"Nothing," she snapped. *"Just get me to Richmond like I asked. I will have the baby somewhere far away and you will never hear from me again."*

"As it is, I wish to God I'd never set eyes on you." Peter wiped his eyes. Sporadic moisture blew into their faces, the small roof over the seat offering scant protection from the rain sailing on gusting winds. He clicked at the horses to pick up speed.

Suddenly, a little girl clambered from under the boughs of a huge magnolia. Her skirts caught in the branches, and she twisted to free herself. She fell to the ground as the wagon barreled toward her. The driver tugged the reins to the right, and the horses veered in that direction. As a thunderclap resounded, lightning filled the sky with an unearthly greenish glow. The child stood frozen in the path and as they moved forward, the driver reached out and grabbed the girl with one hand, dragging her to the seat.

The little girl cried out, then huddled under the protective arm of the driver. She clutched the doll to her chest, but the watch slid from her fingers to the wagon floor.

The maid bent forward and picked up the timepiece. As the driver eased up on the reins, she screamed, *"Don't stop!"*

"We have to," he shouted.

"Keep going, Peter." The maid's voice took on a steely tone as she withdrew a small pistol from the folds of her skirt and pressed it to the whimpering child's temple.

Peter's eyes widened in horror while Margaret's squinted shut as the cold steel dug into her eyebrow.

Eerie green lighting crackled across the sky in time with the burst of thunder. Peter gripped the reins to control the skittish horse. A whirlwind of dirt and rain raised the wagon and animal into a spin.

When the twirling ended, the wooden cart dropped to the ground and spun once in the dirt, landing on a street in Civil War-era Richmond, Virginia.

Peter McGowan remained at the reins but beside him, the bench was empty.

Little Margaret Lawrence twirled through a tunnel of lights and whooshing air on her way to colonial Richmond, where a woman named Abigail Rocher bargained with a seedy man for the services of a child servant.

And the unscrupulous maid CarlyAnna Chambers landed in a jewelry shop in 21st century Richmond, selling an antique watch to a seedy jeweler to finance the start of a new life.

Modern Day Portsmouth, Virginia

In spite of the tension exuding from every corner of the room, exhaustion threatened to overtake the occupants. While Chase and Mary Jo, Terry and Kyle, and Stephanie and Gage sat near each other in chairs or on the floor, Sandi and Kirby remained apart. He still sat on the brick ledge of the hearth while she settled in one corner of the couch. Margaret lay awake, unblinking and silent, with her head resting on Sandi's lap and her gaze remained locked on the clock near Kirby's shoulder.

The minute hand clicked its way to twelve o'clock, tolling an uneventful midnight hour.

"Listen, everybody," Terry said when the last chime clanged. She straightened in her chair. At her feet, Kyle shifted his position, head tilted back against the arms of chair. His eyelids drooped.

Terry continued, "We've all been managing our daily lives on only a few hours of sleep, and this whole ordeal has drained us, emotionally and physically. We can take turns resting, until something happens."

"Who can sleep?" Stephanie yawned, setting off a chain reaction around the room.

"If you stay awake, fine. Let's just plan that Kyle and I will take first watch. If we get too sleepy, we'll tag someone at two. Whoever has that watch can wake us all just before three. If nothing happens, we return to normal schedules and look for more clues."

Gage removed a plump throw pillow from the chair he leaned against and tucked it behind his head. He drew Stephanie into the curve of his arm. "I wouldn't mind a little shut-eye. I've got to report for duty at eight."

Chase yawned for a second time, and said, "I've got to meet the owners of the new craft whiskey distillery at six to get started on their remodel job."

"What an ungodly hour to do business," Mary Jo remarked as she stifled a yawn.

Chase bumped her leg. "This from she who arrives at her café at six a.m. to bake French pastry thingies."

Mary Jo scooted from the chair and nestled beside her fiancé. "And this from the man who is first in line to buy them."

"Yeah, I do like your honey buns," Chase answered

with a mischievous grin.

"I don't serve honey buns in—oh, you're very clever, slick."

After the laughter, the room grew quiet, save for the ticking clock and the steady breathing of the first ones of the group to fall asleep. Terry withdrew her phone from her pocket and scrolled to her games, adding the sounds of light tapping as her fingers raced over her keyboard.

The minutes passed and emitted the single toll that marked each quarter of the hour. As the arrows made their journey toward the one o'clock position, the sounds of sleep permeated the room. A cacophony of soft breathing provided background music to Mary Jo's light snores. Her head lolled back on the cushion, her mouth slack. She sat with her back against the chair, her arms crossed at her chest, her long legs crossed at the ankles. Chase had stretched out on his stomach nearby, head pillowed in his arms.

Terry suppressed a giggle as she aimed her phone and took pictures of everyone who slept. Besides her, only Kirby and Margaret remained awake.

"Future blackmail," she whispered to Kirby, unable to hold back the giggle this time.

Margaret slipped from her place beside Sandi and came over to the fireplace to sit beside Terry. She held tight to Norrie's doll as she sat beside her and stared at the cell phone. She managed a weak smile in Kirby's direction.

Terry instinctively aimed the phone camera and took a selfie with Margaret. She then scrolled through to the picture and showed it to the girl.

Margaret pointed to Kirby and Terry nodded. He knelt beside the chair and she stood beside him, angling her head to touch his. They were too close to her screen and

Terry waggled her fingers to get them to move a little further away.

The clock chimed one o'clock as the three posed for more pictures, some with silly faces. Their snickers grew louder. The others stirred and eventually woke up.

Margaret insisted on having a picture taken with each one of the adults. Terry then showed her how to swipe her finger across the screen to bring up each picture. It took a few tries before Margaret got the hang of it and she kept repeating the moves, laughing at the silly pictures and talking in a low voice to each grown-up as she showed them her picture with them.

Mary Jo made a fresh pot of coffee, then a second. The time clicked past two-thirty. A distant roll of thunder rattled outside.

"It feels like we are in the waiting room of the hospital, like that night Mom got sick," Gage said. "Waiting for word on how she was."

"Ugh, I had a worse thought," Stephanie added with a shiver. "To me it feels like that hour you sit around waiting before you have to leave for a funeral." Less than a year had passed since the deaths of her parents in a car crash.

A crackle of lightning creased the sky, reflecting in the mirror. Gage circled his arm protectively around her shoulders.

"It's that proverbial pregnant pause," Kyle suggested in an attempt to lighten the mood.

Kirby winced, then glanced toward Sandi. She took a sip from a mug, eyes directed at the liquid inside, then turned her head away from him.

Terry, her back to Sandi and unaware of the tension, popped a pillow alongside Kyle's head. "Keep your proverbial thoughts to yourself, Professor."

Mary Jo stacked empty coffee cups and saucers on the tray and asked, "Anyone ready for another pot of coffee?"

"Not me, I've had too much caffeine as it is, so excuse me while I run to the bathroom." Stephanie scrambled to her feet and headed toward the tiny powder room in the hall.

"Not me." Terry stood and stretched. "If anyone is inclined for a bathroom run, now is the time," she suggested as she pulled Kyle to his feet. "Sandi, I'll use the bathroom in the innkeeper's suite, if you don't mind. Meet y'all back here in a few."

"Right behind ya, babe," Kyle said.

The others quietly moved around the room or stretched in place. Once again, the most prominent sound in the room was the clock ticking the minutes away.

When another crack of lightning flashed, Margaret inched closer to Kirby. The resounding thunderclap followed almost immediately. Small glass bric-a-brac rattled in place.

Stephanie returned to the parlor, picked up Nicole's colonial doll and carried it to the chair she had been sitting in earlier.

Just as she sat, the hands of the heirloom mantle clock clicked into the 2:58 position. Instead of the single chime announcing the quarter hour, a long, hollow clang resounded, reverberating through every metal piece in the room. The candlesticks trembled as the clang echoed from their bases. The clock hands whirled backwards, the internal metal gears grating and amplifying each time the big hand passed twelve.

A flurry of activity whirled around the room. Pages in books and magazines flipped open. Throw cushions levitated and spun like planets orbiting the sun. A small ceramic box rose and fell to the floor, shattering and spilling the peppermints stored within.

The mirror quivered and puffed as wind blew in and out of the glass.

Margaret screamed as the grainy whirlwind tried to pull Norrie's doll from her arms, while another wispy tentacle tried to take the doll from Stephanie. She caught the foot of the heirloom colonial doll as the winds ripped it from her hands and she hugged it close to her chest. Sandi jumped to her feet and stood before the mirror, shouting Norrie's name

Mary Jo raced into the room. Chase grabbed her arm but she shook it off and ran to Stephanie's side, Chase right behind her.

The next lightning bolt seemed to shoot right into the parlor, and the subsequent thunder jarred the floor under their feet.

The mirror glass separated as if a giant mouth opened. A multi-colored mist shot forth and swathed Kirby and Margaret, drawing them inside. Gage and Chase tried to grab Kirby's feet but the man and child disappeared into the void.

A tentacle of the swirling wind reached for Stephanie. Gage shielded her with his body but the haze enveloped her feet, then Mary Jo's. Chase added his weight as anchor, but like liquid being sucked into a straw, both women spun from the men's grasp and vanished head-first into the mirror.

As quickly as it all began, the commotion stopped. The noise ended, the lights returned to normal, and the rattling knickknacks settled in place.

The clock's hands slowed but continued to turn backwards. Above, the mirror puffed in short pulses.

Terry and Kyle strolled back into the room.

"Almost time…" She stopped as she looked around the room and at the stunned faces of the remaining occupants.

"The mirror took Stephanie, Kirby, Mary Jo, and the kid," Gage snapped. "Didn't you hear all the commotion? All the thunder, lightning? The stuff moving around?"

"No, we didn't hear anything. The rest of the house was silent. We thought we had time before three o'clock."

"Oh, God, please let them find Norrie," Sandi prayed. "Why didn't I go this time?"

"Why didn't I get to go?" Terry ran to the fireplace and reached a hand toward the mirror. Her fingertips pushed through the glass.

"Don't touch anything," Kyle warned.

Terry turned, fingers on the frame of the mirror. "I guess I missed the chance to go." She pushed one of the silver candlesticks back in place. Sparks shot from her fingers.

The clock chimed the first of the three tolls.

The mirror mouth opened once again, vacuuming her into the abyss.

The last of the supernatural activity ended.

Left behind in stunned silence were Gage, Chase, Kyle—and Sandi.

CHAPTER 7

Stephanie
Somewhere in Time

Stephanie floated through a brilliant bluish tunnel. All around her, tiny red, blue, and green lights circled her body, flickering on and off like multi-colored fireflies. She sailed along, airy as a feather on the wind. The sensation of weightlessness gave her a sense of freedom she had never experienced before. She stretched into a pirouette pose, one arm curved gracefully over her head and the other clutching Nicole's colonial doll tight to her chest.

She swept her free arm through the twirling sparkles. Pleasant musical notes tinkled every time she displaced the tiny beams.

Childish giggles, as melodic as the musical notes, added to the pleasant aura.

Have I died and gone to heaven? The realization that she may have left Gage behind sent a wave of sadness through her.

The tunnel darkened a bit. Her weight grew heavy and she dropped a few inches from her lofty position. She looked down toward her feet, where the bright lights narrowed as it spiraled to a funnel large enough for her body to fall through. Sparkles circled her shoulders and under her arms, and she ascended a few inches.

A single, slightly larger white light darted back and forth in front of her face, growing brighter each time it zipped by.

Stephanie smiled, and immediately some of the heaviness left her and she floated a few inches higher.

"Are you trying to tell me not to be sad?" she asked the beam. The tiny circle pulsed as it performed loop-the-loops, traces of light following the pattern in its wake.

The light drifted close to her nose. Stephanie's eyes crossed as her gaze followed its movement. A giggle escaped from her lips and she floated further above the dark abyss.

"Do you want me to laugh?" Stephanie asked. The light bounced with excitement, glowing contrails lingering in the path.

Juvenile titters gave way to girlish laughter.

"Will I go home again?" Stephanie asked, performing another pirouette. The guiding sparkle moved with her, always inches from her nose until it bounced off.

"Okay." Stephanie laughed, and the unseen mirth echoed. "I think you are telling me to trust you." The last of the weight dropped from her body.

The white globe shot forward and swirled before it zipped back to Stephanie's nose, then away again, pausing expectantly. It bounced in place, and Stephanie could have sworn the beam looked back at her.

"I'm coming." Stephanie called. She spoke but the words came forth on a musical tone.

With three grand *jeté* leaps—a feat a pre-teen Stephanie could never accomplish in her ballet class—she sailed through the void and caught up with the guiding light.

Doors opened and closed as Stephanie followed the

guiding light along the never-ending corridor. She took advantage of the lack of gravity, rolling forward in an airy willowy somersault, then she straightened and pointed her toes downward, spin slowing as she came to a standstill. She hovered for a moment before arching her back and spinning in a backwards flip.

A set of double doors opened, and a gentle pull drew her inward, as a magnet would attract metal. She floated to the entrance, stopping to peer into a room so bright that she could not ascertain what was inside.

The guiding beam stopped just short of the threshold, buzzed around Stephanie's head and skidded again to a stop.

"Are you going with me?" Stephanie asked.

In answer, the minuscule beam moved closer and brushed Stephanie's nose in an Eskimo kiss.

The sparkles and lights faded, and Stephanie was sucked past the twin doors, which promptly slammed shut behind her.

As her eyes adjusted to the glare, she looked down and saw a planked floor below her.

Gravity took over and she plummeted downward. She landed on her feet, but the impact buckled her knees and her legs folded beneath her at the foot of an ornate four-poster bed. She grabbed the bedstead and drew herself to a kneeling position.

A woman and a girl of about ten stood near the head of the carved headboard, flickering candles illuminating their sad faces. The girl held the right hand of the ill woman.

"Come, Emily, we must let your great-grandmama rest." The woman dabbed a hankie to her eye as she held her other hand toward the little girl.

Stephanie pulled herself upright and made direct eye

contact with an elderly female huddled under the covers. Her clear blue eyes brightened as she smiled toward Stephanie. A dimple appeared in one cheek.

The woman looked in the same direction before turning back. "Do you see something, Grandmama Nicole?"

Nicole! Stephanie sucked in a gasp.

Only the sick woman seemed to notice Stephanie had arrived in the room, but she shook her head. Her voice was hoarse as she shooed the woman and child from her side with a weak wave of her hand. "My darlings, please go get some rest. Geneviève, tend to your family. Leave me be for a while."

"Great-Grandmama, I don't want to leave you," protested the child, her small hand caressing the blue-veined hand of her grandmother.

"I know, Emily darling. But do this just for a while, my little one. I will be fine. Geneviève, ask your papa to come too. Come back at four o'clock."

Stephanie's gaze drew toward a clock on a dressing table. The hands clicked into place at three-thirty.

"Yes, Grandmama." The woman leaned forward and brushed the old woman's cheek with kisses. She walked to the door, her heavy taffeta skirts rustling as she swept wept past Stephanie with not so much as a glance in her direction.

The great-granddaughter lingered before planting a kiss on her grandmother's weathered cheek, then fluffed the coverlet, and dashed toward the door, so close the hem of her dress swished against Stephanie's leg. She stopped short, eyes darting from side to side as she frowned. She waved her hands right through Stephanie. She peered harder, but as her mother's fading voice called her, she followed the grown-up, shutting the door with a gentle click.

Stephanie looked down at her feet, then raised a hand toward the light. Her body was solid, as was the doll tucked in one arm.

The woman in the bed waited until the door closed, then crooked her finger and whispered, "Come closer, child."

Somewhere in time
Mary Jo

Mary Jo's feet touched a solid landing that immediately rocked from side to side. She lost her balance and landed in a supine position, spiraling along a downward corkscrew chute. She raised her hands to steady herself, but the momentum was too great. Gravity pulled her flat on her back as she swayed from side to side on the downhill slide. Each time she banked a curve, she gained speed and rose dangerously close to the edge of the chute.

A cloud of multi-colored lights floated at her feet, dispersing as she crashed through them. The beams regrouped and gathered again, repeating the movements as she descended.

The entire time, one tiny red orb, solid and sparkling, led the way.

In her peripheral vision, doors opened, illuminated by bursts of lights that flashed to the sounds of gunfire. She tried to cover her ears to block out the deafening explosions, but the pull on her body forced her arms to remain flat.

As she spiraled downward toward a black hole, one door crashed against the dark wall and remained open. Smoke billowed out in short puffs. The chute flattened and Mary Jo slid towards the portal.

To keep from sliding further, she grabbed the doorframe in a white-knuckled grip. Her feet passed over the threshold and she hung straight out, like a flag shrouded in a windy fog. She tightened her grip and managed to turn over. She dragged herself forward until her upper body was inside the portal. She hooked one elbow on the doorframe, and then managed to get the opposite leg up for more leverage.

The red light twirled in front of her face. As it touched Mary Jo's nose in a gentle buss, she relaxed her grip.

Suction tugged her body and she popped backwards with the force of a cork exploding from a bottle of champagne. She landed on her back, her shoulders and head absorbing the impact. Stunned, she struggled to breathe as haze trailed past her, a few inches above the ground.

She coughed, sending a painful jolt through her shoulder blades. A second cough bubbled to the surface and she hitched her breath to suppress it.

Her vision cleared and she pushed to her elbows to glance around her.

She sucked in an acrid taste of sulfur that she recognized all too well.

Gunpowder.

The ping of bullets whizzed close by her head as booms—heavy artillery, not thunder—exploded in the distance. She dropped flat on her back, ignoring the sharp stab in her lungs, and rolled over onto her stomach. With her face pressed against the ground, she could feel the vibrations of running feet. Commanding voices shouted orders but the words were lost in the volley of gunfire that followed.

The outline of a long gun barrel took shape in the

floating mist. Raising her head enough to look around, a horrifying thought sent chills through her.

Am I back in Afghanistan?

Terry
Somewhere in Time

A long tunnel of closed doors stretched before Terry, with one open door at the far end awash in shimmering gold light. While gentle musical notes tinkled in the distance, a current of red, white, and green light beams swirled around her. A single blue bulb, brighter than all the others, zipped back and forth between the door and Terry. She extended one arm and the blue beam landed on her finger with the delicate grace of a butterfly. She laughed as she brought her hand closer and blew a gentle kiss toward the light.

One moment, she stood at one end of the corridor.

The next, she sailed through time the same way she sailed through life—full speed ahead. The iridescent glow dispersed as she crashed through and landed flat on her stomach on the other side.

Her eyes adjusted to the light and she recognized a room of familiar objects intermingled with items she had never seen before.

She knew exactly where she was in time—she just didn't know when.

Kirby and Margaret
Somewhere in Time

Margaret screamed. Jolts of electrifying green lights surrounded Kirby as he and Margaret twirled in a vacuum, her tiny hands clenching his neck and Norrie's doll lodged between them. The doll's plastic arm stabbed him under the ribs, but he tightened his grip.

He offered a mental prayer of thanks. Other than the spinning whirlwind carrying him and the frightened girl along, Kirby experienced none of the physical pains his body had endured during his previous time travel.

"Hold on, Margaret, honey," he shouted. Winds thrashed her long hair, sending thick strands across Kirby's mouth. He spat and shook his head as more tendrils slapped his cheek. He turned his face to block the wind and buried his cheek against his shoulder.

Man and child navigated a pulsating tunnel that alternated between endless space and a narrowness through which they could barely pass.

With a pop they emerged from another narrow tube. This time the force ripped Margaret from his arms. She shrieked, arms outstretched as she was pulled into an open doorway. The door slammed shut on her fading scream.

Kirby whirled in place, pivoting like a toy top as a sparkling array of colored lights whirled around him. A single green light emerged from the mix and circled his head. The vortex moved in widening circles, bringing him to the threshold of the same doorway that had taken Margaret.

He tottered on the edge, looking down at a vast expanse of a billowing cloud-like haze before a force of pressure sucked him into the abyss.

CHAPTER 8

Stephanie
New England, 1859

"Come here, child," the old woman said with a wave of her feeble hand.

Stephanie rotated one complete turn as she looked all around her for the child. Then she realized she was the "child" the woman called for. The floors squeaked as she stepped closer to the bed.

"You can see me, Grandmother Nicole?" Stephanie's voice caught in her throat.

"I can. You are different somehow than when I first came to find you."

Stephanie nodded, unsure of how much she should explain. Months earlier, Nicole had appeared to her as a child ghost, begging Stephanie to find her lost teardrop. The ethereal figure never spoke to Stephanie, but communicated through little Tanner, who then relayed messages to Stephanie.

Now Stephanie was back in Nicole's time in some kind of reversed ghost role.

"I never expected to see you again, Grandmother Nicole."

"Nor I you, little one." Nicole's eyes sparkled at sight of the doll. "You have my baby."

Confusion shook Stephanie until she remembered reading that colonial girls usually referred to their dolls as "my baby." She sat on the edge of the bed and nestled the doll beside her ancestress.

"Oh, I missed my baby for so many years." A tear rolled down Nicole's cheek as she hugged the doll. "I cried and cried. Then I forgot about her when I grew up and had children of my own. Where did you find her?"

"I found her hidden away in an attic. Kirby—from my time—is a descendant of your brother Louis. We don't understand what happened, but somehow, he traveled back to your time, and visited with Louis."

Nicole nodded. "And I know I came to your time, but I was not old like I am now. I don't understand how I know this, but I was lost somewhere. Not in the dark, I was always surrounded by pretty lights. But somewhere, and no one could help me. Until you…" She shook her head, blue eyes clouded with confusion.

When Nicole did not speak again, Stephanie continued. "Kirby had many experiences that showed him parts of Louis' younger life, and he saw what happened the night you left the doll behind, when rogue British soldiers attacked your mother and grandfather." Stephanie repeated the stories Kirby had shared. "Kirby helped Louis, freed him from the guilt that bound him here because of what he thought he did to Abigail."

"That was both a wonderful and horrible night." Nicole coughed and struggled to a sitting position. Stephanie reached for a pitcher on the stand beside the bed and poured water into a cup. Her ancestress drank deeply and cleared her throat. She handed the cup back, then smiled as Stephanie plumped a pillow around her before returning to her seat on the edge of the bed.

Nicole tightened her grip on the old doll. Voice a little stronger and with the slightest trace of a French accent, she continued speaking. "I harbored such guilt for many years. You see, I thought God was punishing me for stealing the necklace and that is why my mother died. Finally, the guilt faded away as I grew up. While visiting Mama's cousin in New York, I met and fell in love with a wonderful man, Henri Lebeque. A soldier, of course."

A new energy seemed to come over Nicole. Her eyes brightened. "Henri and I were married on the first day of the new century, January one, eighteen hundred, and two years later we had a baby boy we named Edward Étienne. We moved to Champlain, New York, where Henri had family who had fled Acadia during the expulsion and settled there. One of Mama's cousins lived there as well, but I missed my own family so much. Marie Josephé settled in New England with her family. Louis married Lizzie, and remained in Portsmouth. Theresé and her husband bought a house next door to him. I traveled back to Portsmouth only once, in the spring of eighteen twelve. Papa was ill and had never seen Edward Étienne, who was ten at the time. Papa took us to see the ocean. The carriage ride was so long but it was amazing to see the sun rise over the horizon. Then America declared war on Britain. I believe it was in June of that year. Riots broke out in Baltimore and Henri had to return to his unit. Papa died just before we left, but his last wishes were that he could help the Americans in another battle against Britain. My husband and I, and our son Edward, arrived back home and Henri was immediately dispatched to the war. He soon fought in a battle with the British in a place called Queenston. I never saw him again."

A fresh tear slid down her cheek. "Henri was so

young, not even forty. He died in battle in October of eighteen twelve, in the same battle that killed the British commander Brock. I never married again. There was no one for me but my Henri."

A light rap at the door interrupted Nicole and she settled into silence, another tear trailing down her cheek. In spite of her age, her skin was remarkably smooth.

The woman who had been in the room earlier peeked around the door.

"Grandmother, did you call me?"

"No, Geneviève, I am fine. Has your father arrived?"

"No, Grandmother, but we expect him to be here any moment."

Nicole nodded. "I will rest a bit more, then. Please come back when he arrives."

Geneviève nodded, and closed the door. Stephanie settled her hand over her fluttering heart. Nicole's granddaughter Geneviève would be yet another ancestor to Stephanie.

"How is it you see me and Geneviève does not?" Stephanie asked.

"I do not know. How is it you are able to come to me from the future? Or I to come to as a child into your time?"

"That I do not understand either, Grandmother Nicole. We believe that for some reason you and your sisters and brother did not find true peace in your lives and we are to help you."

"My sisters told me Mama had a gift of a second sight, and how she often talked about seeing people we could not see."

"We believe Tanner—who is a descendant of Therésé and helped you to find when you came to me—we believe he has the gift. He has been the one to help everyone."

"Ah, Tanner is an amazing child. I loved to hear him laugh. Tell me, where did you find my baby? How?"

"On the night the soldiers attacked your family, Louis stayed behind in his role of spy soldier to help your mother and grandfather. He saw the doll and knew it carried the secrets for the American and French armies. He had the maid, Lizzie, hide it. Then it was forgotten for many years. I found it by accident in the old house in Portsmouth, where you appeared to me several times."

Nicole stroked her fingers along the doll's dress. "I always knew about the tiny pocket in the hem of her dress. They thought they were clever to hide the secret papers, but I always knew they were there. I could not read yet, but the notes sometimes had strange drawings in them, and I knew they were important for our father's work. I would peek at the papers, but I was always careful to return them. When I was older, my sisters told me they were always so frightened that I would show the doll to the wrong soldier, who would discover the secret papers and turn us in as spies."

Stephanie nodded. "From what we learned, your father and brother were spies, as was your grandfather Phillip. One of the ways they passed secret messages was to place papers in that pocket. If your sisters learned something that Louis needed to know, they would find him in the market square."

Nicole nodded. "I did not learn of this until many years later." She ran her fingers around the entire hem and frowned.

"I—I..." She shook her head sadly. "I hid my teardrop in this dress. I never saw it again."

"Are you looking for this, Grandmother Nicole?" Stephanie asked. She reached under the collar of her sweater and zipped her finger along the chain until she found the teardrop diamond and lifted it.

Nicole's weathered hands flew to her cheeks. "My teardrop. You found that too? May I see it one more time?" Tears rimmed her eyes.

Stephanie reached behind and fumbled with the clasp of the necklace. She took the chain and transferred the necklace to her sixth great-grandmother's neck and fastened the clip.

Nicole nodded as she tilted her chin and looked at the jewel. More tears splashed on her wrist.

"On my wedding day, Papa gave me another teardrop necklace to replace the one I lost. I treasured that one all these years, but I always grieved for the first, because it reminded me of Mama. She did get to see all of us sisters with our pretty jewels." Nicole fumbled to remove the chain from her neck.

"No, Grandmother Nicole, that is your necklace," Stephanie protested.

"No, my dear," Nicole said. "This is yours now. I do not think you could return to your time without it. I would love to have you stay, but I am not long for this world." She leaned forward and Stephanie unclasped the ends and put the chain back on her neck.

"Thank you, my dear and future granddaughter. You have brought me peace and comfort." Nicole smiled and drew the covers to her chin, her doll propped on the bed beside her.

A light knock on the door startled them both.

All of the energy seemed to fade, and Nicole sank into the pillows.

"Grandmother?" Stephanie leaned forward, swallowing past the lump in her throat. She blinked but could not stop the hot tears from rolling down her cheek.

Nicole patted her hand weakly.

"Grandmama?" The door opened and Genevie stepped in. "Papa is here." She led a tall man into the room. Stephanie backed away from the bed, but the father and daughter sailed past her without a glance in her direction.

"You made it, Edward." Nicole's voice rasped deep in her throat.

"Don't talk, Mama," he said, his voice catching. He knelt by her side and took her hand in his. "Geneviève sent word to me and I came as fast as I could."

"I am glad you came, Edward. I am ready to let go. It is time and I can go in peace now. I love all of you so much, but it hurts to stay."

"Mama..." Edward choked the words as he raised her hand to his cheek. "I don't want you to go, but if you have to, it is all right."

"Don't cry for me, son. I've had a good, wonderful life. You were a joy to me, as are your daughter and granddaughter. My only regret is that your father died so young. But I will see him soon. And my mama and papa are waiting for me. I will come back in the spring. Look for me in the flowers."

At that moment, the little girl Emily called from the door, "May I come in, Mama?"

"Emily, darling, Great-Grandmama is still sick." Geneviève's voice quivered.

Her father raised his head. "She's gone," he whispered, then buried his head into the pillow near his mother's shoulder, his own shoulders heaving with grief. His daughter slipped her arm across his back, sobbing.

Stephanie clapped her hands to her mouth and bit back a sob. The ticking of the clock on the nightstand seemed to grow louder as the hands inched toward the hour.

Emily entered the room and tiptoed to the foot of the bed. She gave a sad sigh as she looked at her grandmother, then eyes widened as her gaze fell on Stephanie.

Edward stood up and heaved a sigh, his face turned to the still form on the bed. He hugged his daughter, and then noticing his granddaughter for the first time, held out his hand. She ran forward, placing an arm around both of them.

"Is Great-Grandmama in heaven now?" Emily asked.

"Yes, she is, honey." Edward lifted her in his arms and hugged her.

"Papa, look." Geneviève gasped and pointed toward the doll. "Where did that come from?"

"Her." Emily picked the doll up and handed it to Stephanie.

Winds roared past Stephanie's ears and the floor quivered under her feet.

By the time the clock struck, she and the doll were gone.

CHAPTER 9

Peter and Liana
Somewhere in time

Liana slid to the floor. The rectangle of light appeared and disappeared, leaving her with an afterimage of its shape in the dark, even when she closed her eyes.

"So, we are lost in time? Is that all we see, just that box of light coming and going?" she asked.

"Yup." Peter's voice reverberated somewhere to her left. "It's brighter at some times than others. Sometimes I hear voices on the other side, and once or twice I've even seen a vague image through the opening. By the time I reach it, it moves. Or disappears."

His paced back and forth, his footsteps echoing in the chamber. "Then one day, the light looked different. I can't explain it. More colorful, maybe, like sparkles of color. Reds and greens and blues. Then this black chamber flashed in a brilliant white and it seemed like the bones were being pulled right out of my body. I twisted and turned through all these swirling lights and landed right where I found you. I could see you, I could follow you, but you couldn't see me. At least not right away. I saw you do that crazy stuff to the doll and to the clothes. You must have been pretty mad at someone to do what you did."

"Oh, what would you know about it?" Liana snapped.

"Oh, I know plenty, believe me." Peter knelt close to Liana and hissed in her ear. *"I've wanted to break you with my bare hands ever since you left me to suffer the consequences of your criminal acts."*

Mary Jo
Yorktown, 1781

Artillery boomed in the distance, moving much closer to Mary Jo. Bullets whizzed nearby. As the haze rolled around her, she raised her head slightly, able only to see low to the ground. As the hazed lifted and she had clearer vision, her jaw dropped and she blinked her eyes.

She saw herself, dressed in a tattered colonial dress and apron. All around her, smoking cannons thundered. She shoved a ramrod down the barrel of one as a soldier on the opposite side fired a musket into hazy puffs of smoke rolling past. The soldier, dressed in a blue jacket and tan breeches, clutched his chest.

I must be hallucinating! How many times had she had the same dream, of being on a battlefield surrounded by cannons and heavy gunfire? Hundreds of times in her life—at the least.

Mary Jo shook her head and opened her eyes to the same view. It *was* the colonial war dream again, something she had not had for months.

Or she was living the nightmare.

There were slight variations in the dreams as changing events in her life occurred, but always included her engaged in battle or tending to a wounded soldier, sometimes in a modern war and sometimes back in colonial times.

The visions had intensified after her return from the real-life war in Afghanistan. While traveling in a supply convoy, the various vehicles kept breaking down and the third time they stalled, they were sitting ducks. Two rocket-propelled grenades tore through their line, decimating the vehicle ahead of them and heavily damaging the one she was in.

Her driver, Madison North, received the most critical injuries and died in her arms, making her promise to deliver a message to his mother and to make peace with her own. Once she had fulfilled her promises to her dying Army colleague, the painful dreams had finally ended.

A bullet whizzed past and a body fell right in front of her. Blood splattered across her face and she stared into the lifeless eyes of a dead soldier in blue coat with brass buttons. Another cloud of haze enveloped the area.

This was not a dream or a memory, this was happening right in front of her. Right now.

The haze cleared and she stared. Unlike her dreams, she was not standing at the cannon—but her spitting image was. Her ancestress, Marie Josephé, labored at the cannon and stepped back a pace. The gunner primed the weapon and shouted, "*Amorcé!*"

Mary Jo clearly understood the French word for "primed." This was no dream, and this was not Afghanistan.

This was a colonial battlefield and it was happening. *Now.*

Marie Josephé covered her ears as the gunner lit the powder in the touch hole and yelled, "*Feu.*" The heavy artillery rocked backwards from the force of the explosion.

Mary Jo's ears rang with the impact of the detonation. A high-pitched ringing and internal pressure in her ears caused a momentary deafness to all other sound. Smoke blocked her view again, and she held her breath to avoid the sulfuric taste. She scooted on her stomach in the military low crawl, and bumped into a solid object. Smoke cleared enough for her to see the form of another soldier. She slithered over his body and moved closer to the cannon.

The gunner covered the touch hole with the leather thumb sheath and shouted, "*Prêt.*" Mary Jo's French comprehension kicked in. "Ready."

Marie Josephé prepared the cannon for the next shot.

"I can help." Mary Jo stood and spoke in French.

"Please, we need your help," Marie Josephé shouted in English. She jutted an elbow toward the long-handled wood pole with a cork-screw device at the end. "Push that worm into the barrel and twist it twice to make sure the cannon is clean before we fire the next round."

Mary Jo followed her directions. Along the ridge, other cannons discharged. Echoing firepower landed far to the left and right, shots returned from unseen British forces hunkered behind the redoubt. From the mists, a young soldier ran forward and stood ready with the powder charge.

"*Chargez!*" the gunner gave the command to load. As soon as Marie Josephé loaded it and began ramming, the soldier raced to the rear for another cannonball, which he rolled into the muzzle. Marie Josephé repeated the ramming actions.

The gunner then used a long bar with a sharpened point to poke through the touchhole to expose the powder charge in the bore. Using a tube fashioned from a feather quill, he poured gunpowder to prime the charge, and shouted "*Amorce!*"

"*Prêt.*" Ready. Mary Jo, the young soldier, and Marie Josephé stepped back from their positions in unison and covered their ears.

"*Feu!*" The gunner touched the linstock with a slow match to the touchhole and lit the charge.

They continued these maneuvers until the young soldier shouted that there were no more cannonballs.

It was only then that Mary Jo became aware that there were no sounds of battle. Cannon no longer thundered, and the barrage of rifle bullets had halted. The soldiers turned curious eyes toward Mary Jo, taking in her unconventional clothes. Mari Josephé spoke, in a voice so quiet and rapid that Mary Jo could not keep up with the French conversation.

At that moment, a horse and cavalryman burst through the tree line and raced toward the troops scattered across the field. The rider shouted in English, "We have captured the redoubts. Between the two assaults, almost two hundred British and Hessian soldiers were also captured."

The message was repeated in French. Cheers erupted and weary soldiers came from around bunkers or cannons and met in the field, shaking hands.

The haphazardly-formed cannon crew paired off, the men walking in one direction, Marie Josephé and Mary Jo in the other. They checked among the prostrate soldiers for signs of life. Other weary soldiers came forward with stretchers, ready to start the arduous task of burying the dead.

"Come with me," Marie Josephé said, taking Mary Jo by the arm and guiding her toward a path in the tree line. "We will go to the camp but I want to talk to you first. How is this possible? I did not expect that I would ever see you again."

Mary Jo said, "Nor I you. We have had some strange events happen in my time, and it has sent us all—places. I am here now, but I don't know where the others have gone. I don't believe in ghosts or time travel, yet here I am."

Marie Josephé nodded. "The doctor from your time came here too. He went with Louis to tend to the wounded."

"He has already returned home. I can't explain what is happening, but when we travel back to your time, we seem to be here to fix something that will help your spirits find peace."

"Do you travel in the same way that I came to you? Through the little boy Tanner? I don't know how it happened. It was as if one day he called to me in my mind and I came to your time."

Mary Jo dropped to a fallen tree and sighed. "No, it did not work that way for me to come to you. I don't even know what happened or how I came to be here, but there is a mirror that seems to be a doorway to other worlds. We know that Kirby helped Louis. Our theory is that you and your sisters need us to help you pass to the other side."

In the far distance, cheers rose. Marie Josephé smiled, which faded quickly. "The war is finally over. There will be celebrations today, but we lost so many soldiers. And many more were severely injured."

She sat beside her future granddaughter, and in the same manner, heaved a great sigh. "It was amazing to travel to your time. I saw so many things that we have never even dreamed could exist. I wish I could have stayed longer."

"I do too."

"You fired the cannon as well as a soldier."

"Maybe because I am a soldier." Mary Jo smiled.

"Women are soldiers in your time?"

"Yes, we are. And women pretty much do any job they

want, even those considered to be 'man's work.' It isn't always easy, but most women can study and learn any trade they wish."

"I often dreamed of being a soldier and fighting the British. I hate them!"

Mary Jo smiled again. "Then perhaps I shouldn't tell you that you married an Englishman."

"Never!" Marie Josephé stood and stomped her foot. Then she sat again. "Who is this Englishman?"

Mary Jo had an answer, thanks to the genealogy research Stephanie and Kyle had compiled. "You will meet him in a few years. Your youngest child—and only son—is my ancestor."

"How can I marry an Englishman when we have been fighting them for so long?"

"Not every British citizen was against America during your time," Mary Jo replied with a shrug. "Great Britain is one of our greatest allies now—well, now meaning in my time. And France remains a staunch ally." She spent the next few minutes explaining the outcome of the Revolutionary War and how it had affected the children of Étienne when the soldiers had attacked his wife and his father.

After hearing the story, Marie Josephé shook her head in confusion. "This is all too much for me. I wonder if I have suffered a serious injury that is making my mind play tricks on me. I have seen it happen to the soldiers when they suffer from delirium. They imagine impossible things, like me falling in love with and marrying an Englishman."

May Jo yawned and stretched her arms. She had lost all sense of time. Out of habit, she glanced at her watch. The face was cracked and the hands were stuck at two-fifty-five. She tapped the dial several times, and the second hand suddenly started ticking again. Inching toward three o'clock, like her last memory of standing in front of the mantle clock and watching the time click past.

Looking up, she said, "I may not have much time remaining here. Is there anything else I can answer for you?"

Marie Josephé shook her head, then touched her hand to her neck. "My mother showed me a necklace Papa and Grandpapa had planned to give to me. I lost it somewhere that night the soldiers attacked. Did anyone ever find it?"

Mary Jo stood and reached for the chain around her neck. She unfastened it and handed it to the colonial girl.

"My heart—my ruby heart." Tears spilled down Marie Josephé's cheeks as she placed the chain around her neck. "I did not have time to give it back to Mama. We had to hurry to leave the house. Nicole and I lost our necklaces there. Mama gave the pouch to Louis, and when we were finally reunited, only Theresé's necklace remained in the pouch." She touched the stone.

"After the storm hit, we needed to have many repairs done. I was digging a new garden and found your necklace. It was the day you appeared and told me to dig deep to find my heart."

"And did you, Mary Jo? Did you find your heart?"

"Eventually. I did as you said, not only digging deep to find your ruby heart buried in the dirt, but within myself to find my own peace. I fulfilled my promise to my friend Madison, renewed my relationship with my mother, and found love again with Chase."

Marie Josephé grinned. "The boy Chase. I always liked him."

"Me too. Well, except for a few years when I was mad

at him."

"It is our red hair. Mama said it gave me my temper." Marie Josephé took the pendant off and placed it around her future granddaughter's neck, then kissed her cheek. "Thank you for giving me back my heart, Mary Jo, and for all your family has done to help us find our peace."

The two women embraced and stood back. Marie Josephé wiped a tear from her eye, and touched the finger to a teardrop sliding down Mary Jo's face.

Mary Jo glanced again at her watch.

The minute hand snapped to the hour and she disappeared from the eighteenth century.

CHAPTER 10

Modern Day Portsmouth, Virginia
Naval Medical Center Portsmouth

"Hey, Murphy, you awake?" A doctor in scrubs poked his head around the door and called to his colleague stretched out on a cot.

"Well, I am now." Lt. Commander Murphy O'Shea stretched and yawned.

"Hey, sorry, man, I didn't know you were sleeping."

"It's okay. I just crashed for a few minutes. What's up, Doc?"

Both men chuckled as Murph's co-worker Lieutenant Commander Herbie Jenkins stepped into the room.

"Do you know when Kirby Lawrence comes back from leave?" he asked.

Murph scrubbed his stubble and stood. "Not sure when he comes back. Maybe ten days or so. Why? Is it about one of his patients?"

"No, but it is kind of weird. The foreman of the construction crew that's repairing the windows in Building One came by and brought this." He held up a yellowed envelope with Kirby's full name and rank written across the front. "Said they found it when they came in this morning, and they brought it to our office. I tried calling Kirby but keep getting his voice mail."

"Looks old as hell," Murph remarked as he squinted at the neat script writing.

Herbie shrugged. "Guess it got wet or something."

"It could be important. Soon as I make my rounds, I'm getting out of here, so I'll take it. I think he's been staying at this Bed and Breakfast in Olde Towne. If he's not there I can check with his new lawyer friend. Her office is next door to the B and B." Murphy washed his face at the basin and reached for a towel.

"What happened to that gal he was seeing? The jeweler? Man, she was a looker." Herbie plumped the pillow on the cot and shook out the blanket all at the same time as he kicked off his shoes.

Murph shrugged. "Dunno. He mentioned they broke up, but I don't know any deets."

"Ooh, maybe I can check her out if they broke up. I always thought she gave me the eye." Herbie stretched out on the cot.

"You think every woman is giving you the eye." Murph tossed the damp towel. It landed on Herbie's forehead with a dull flop.

Dr. Herbie Jenkins was already asleep.

Murphy shook his head. He tucked the mysterious letter in his jacket pocket. If he was lucky, he would be leaving after he made his rounds.

Only two hours later than his shift was supposed to end.

All in all, a good day.

Terry
Somewhere in time

Terry floated upward. Her body faced down as she drifted higher and higher, until her back bumped the ceiling like a helium balloon breaking from its tether and reaching a barrier.

A heavy dull drone invaded her ears. Weightless and hovering, she glanced down at the dark room below her, lit only by candles in sconces on the wall or by occasional flashes of lightning.

She recognized the hallway of Clothiste's Inn, with its three doors leading to the bedrooms, two on the left, one on the right. At the far end of the hall was the narrow doorway leading to the attic. On the opposite end was the landing and staircase leading downstairs.

But something was amiss, and it took her a minute to recognize what it was.

She was in the house she knew as a bed and breakfast, but the old-fashioned furnishings were not the same. The doors did not have the modern brass markers depicting the room's décor.

Her ears popped, as one's ears did when ascending to a higher altitude. A crash of thunder preceded the shouts that drifted from the bedroom which should bear the plaque identifying it as the Colonial Room.

"You cannot just kill." A French-accented voice said.

"Of course I can. I shall kill twice tonight." This woman's voice, low and ominous, bore a trace of a British accent. "But I see I should have started with you."

A woman in an old-fashioned nightgown backed out of a bedroom and into the hall. She continued walking backwards until she stumbled into the edge of a small table, the corned jabbing her spine. She pressed one limp hand against her stomach. A narrow strip of cloth from shoulder to wrist acted as a sling for her injured arm.

An older woman in black emerged from the door. A

flash of lightning crackled outside of the hall window, illuminating the woman's pinched face.

As the injured woman steadied herself with her good arm, her hand brushed against a candleholder. Another thunderclap boomed, muffling the sound of the candle falling as she forced the unlit taper to the side. Her fingers closed around the base of the silver stand.

Terry recognized the familiar candleholder. The same silver candlestick and its twin graced the mantle of the fireplace in Clothiste's Inn—in the 21st century.

She recognized the women too. She had once been transported to the past with the ghost of Therésé. The last time she could not hear the conversation between Clothiste and Abigail

Now shivers coursed through Terry at the evil in the woman's tone.

"I tried already to kill you, you know." Abigail's lips curled into a thin smile. "Subtly. Little drops of laudanum here and there in your tea or soup, so no one could detect anything. I should have emptied the bottle and rid myself of you long ago."

"Why do you hate us so?" Clothiste asked. "We have done nothing to you."

"Are you not a woman of French blood? That is all I need to hate you." Abigail stepped closer. "But Phillip—I thought I had won him over. He was as English as I— except for the vile blood in his veins. He called on his solicitor to discuss changing his will. Did you know that? Your daughters will get it all. I will get nothing. But I will not let that happen. I will kill you now, and then him."

Terry sensed the sheer willpower from which her colonial grandmother drew a sudden burst of strength as she swung the candlestick with all the force she could muster. Clothiste came up short, and the square base just grazed Abigail's jaw before Clothiste lost strength and dropped the heavy silver stand.

Abigail's shriek pierced the quiet, and she lunged in rage.

"Stop!" Terry shouted, her voice resounding in her ears. She flailed her arms as she tried to force her body down to stop the fight, but to no avail. Neither woman below seemed to hear or see her.

Clothiste's limp arm flailed at her side as she grabbed Abigail's throat with her good hand. Abigail broke free and pounced, knocking Clothiste into a sitting position on the short hallway table. Clothiste's head cracked against the wall as she drew her knee to her chest and thrust her foot into Abigail's stomach. Abigail shuffled backwards from the blow. Clothiste struggled to step around her toward the bedroom, but Abigail recovered quickly and clutched at her from behind, striking the injured shoulder.

Clothiste flinched and spun around, using her good hand to rake her nails across Abigail's neck. The two women locked in a ruthless embrace, bounced against the wall, spinning back across the hallway to the opposite wall, and into the short banister at the top of the steps.

The wood splintered but held.

Lightning flashed simultaneously with a burst of thunder that shook the house as the two women teetered near the stairwell. They shifted to one side, clawing at each other, their balance shifting as they changed directions.

"Grandmother Clothiste!" Terry shouted helplessly from her hovering perch. She reached her hands downward in a futile attempt to offer help and saw the floor through her outlined limbs.   She was transparent.

I'm a ghost?

The next thunderclap drowned out the thud as Clothiste tumbled down the steps.

Abigail slipped on the top stair and crumpled into a grotesque position.

Far in the distance, a clock tolled.

The scene below Terry shrunk to a pin dot before she was plunged into another whirling frenzy through the tunnel. The wind screeched in her ears as she shot forward into a new scene where she now looked down on the parlor of Clothiste's Inn.

But she was no longer in the eighteenth century—nor had she returned to her own time. By the lighting and furniture in the room, and the clothing of its lone occupant, Terry was clearly in the middle of the nineteenth century.

An old woman sat in a high-back rocker near a dwindling fire, a large crocheted square of blue yarn pooled at her feet. Pretty curtains tied back at the picture window frame let in waning sunlight. She shivered, looked around her, and drew her shawl closer. Then she piled the needles on top of the crocheted material, reached for a cane at her side, and stood.

"I know you are here. I feel you." Although the woman's voice had aged, Terry recognized it was Theresé speaking to the otherwise empty room.

"I'm here, Grandmother Theresé," Terry called. Her voice warbled, as if bubbling through water. "Look up. I'm here above you."

Seconds later, Theresé moved toward the fireplace and reached for the poker. With surprisingly strong motions, she stoked the embers until new flames licked the logs. She drew a long wooden match from a copper container and touched the tip to the fire. With the lit match, she reached for one of the silver candlesticks and lit the wick of a pale blue candle. She moved the match to its mate.

When she put her hand on the base of the second candlestick, the parlor exploded in bright flashes. A filmy scene enveloped the room, as if projecting a black and white movie that replicated the same scenes Terry had just witnessed, where Clothiste had struck Abigail across the chin with the silver candle stand. The grainy image repeated the violent struggle between them, just as before.

Theresé screamed and knocked the candlestick from the mantle. She dropped the match into the fireplace and backed away.

"Great-grandmama!" A voice called as the door burst open and a young woman raced to Theresé side, followed by another about the same age.

"Take them away, Celestine, take them away." Theresé's voice quivered as her shaking hands pointed to the floor. Then she cast nervous glances around the room. "Where is she? Where is she?"

"What is it, Great-grandmama? What are you talking about? Who are you talking about?" The women, in late teens or early twenties, helped Therese to the chair.

"They are evil, get them out of here. Take them away and destroy them."

Celestine turned to the other girl and said, "Louisa, take the candlesticks out of here. Tell Frank that Grandmother had another episode and have him put them away. They are upsetting her horribly for some reason."

"Don't touch them!" Therese screamed.

"She has to pick them up to get them out of here, Great-grandmama." Celestine smoothed the older woman's shawl as she looked over her shoulder and nodded to Louisa. The latter grabbed the candlesticks without incident and scurried from the room.

"Where is she? Where is Terry?"

"Who is Terry, Grandmama?"

"My granddaughter. My other granddaughter."

Celestine sucked her breath in. "It is just I here, Grandmama. Louisa removed the candlesticks. Everything is in order now. Can I get you some hot tea, or something to sooth you?"

"Yes, I would like some tea." Therese's voice was calm as she patted Celestine's hand.

"Are you sure? Perhaps I should stay with you until Emily returns."

"I am fine, dear. My old mind is just playing tricks on me. I am fine. Please, go fetch me a lovely cup of tea." She shooed the young woman away.

Celestine nodded, walked backwards to the door, her gaze on her great-grandmother. She then closed the door behind her as she exited.

Weight returned to Terry's body and her solid form drifted to the floor to kneel in front of Therese.

"I am here, Grandmother Therese. Can you see me now?"

"I knew you were here. I could feel you; but I could not see you."

Terry placed her hands over the thin blue-veined hands of her ancestress and said, "I do not know what is happening, Grandmother. I have now come to your time, as you did to mine."

Therese nodded. "It is nearly finished, my child. My sisters have found peace, and I am ready to leave this world—the real world—one last time. Louis is at peace, but you must get the child Margaret back to her time before it is too late, else this cycle of unrest will begin again."

"Do you mean that the other jewels will remain lost?

You know about Margaret? How can you know all of this, Grandmother Theresé?" Terry touched the gold cross with the blue sapphire that dangled from the chain. "Is it the necklace, Grandmother? Do you need this back?" She reached behind her neck to unclasp the hook.

Theresé shook her head. "I never had to search for my True Color, Terry. I never lost it. But the others have to find their peace before they can rest eternally. Help them if you can." She held Terry's hand to her weathered cheek and kissed her knuckles.

She stood and brushed a kiss across her grandmother's cheek. "Goodbye, Grandmother Theresé," she whispered over the lump in her throat.

Theresé nodded once and smiled weakly, her blue eyes clouding as the life faded from her eyes and her head tilted to her shoulder.

Tears of sadness welled in Terry's eyes and trailed down her cheek. The mantle clock tolled the first chime of the hour and her hands began the transition to transparency once again.

The door opened and Celestine returned with a tray. Her eyes grew wide as her gaze drifted to the chair. The tray dropped to the floor with a clatter. China teacups and saucers shattered, the teapot flipped to its side, spilling the hot water.

"Oh, no, Grandmama, no, no!" Celestine rushed to her grandmother as Terry floated upward.

By the time the clock finished its third toll, Theresé's soul and Terry's body had left the room.

Or so Terry thought. As she shot through the vortex of flashing lights and emerged onto the other side, she found herself floating near the ceiling of the same hallway, descending to the floor. Somewhat different décor graced the room, but she knew she was once again back in the house in an era long before it had been converted into Clothiste's Inn.

On a table on one wall, a Victorian oil lamp provided light. Terry recognized the brass lamp with pink and red roses painted on a porcelain base and hurricane chimney. The same lamp now graced "The Antebellum" room of the inn in the twenty-first century.

An older woman sat in a wheelchair—but this woman was neither Theresé nor near death. Her left leg was set in a splint, wrapped in bandages and propped up on the footrest. Her voluminous satin skirt rustled as she tapped her good foot and clapped her hands in time with the music.

Two boys, obviously twins, scrambled up the stairs, tripping over each other as they raced toward the wheelchair.

A little girl followed at a demure pace until she reached the top step and then she broke into a run, passing her brothers with her arms outstretched. "We came to say goodnight, Grandma!"

"Oh, come to me, my darling little Maggie. And my Frank and Jack." The nearly identical twins hopped on either side of the chair and kissed her cheek.

Maggie! Terry sucked in a breath and peered closer. Margaret—the same Margaret who had traveled to the 21st century—smiling fresh-faced and dressed in nightclothes, hugged her grandmother. Terry racked her brain, wishing Stephanie was here to list the lineage of the family tree. One of those twin boys was Kirby's great-great-grandfather, but she had no idea which was which.

The soulful wail of bagpipes drifted up the stairs.

"Oh, the Highland Fling!" Margaret jumped to her feet and stood in front of her grandmother's chair, heels together and toes pointed outward. She fisted her hands on her hips, bowed at the waist and held the pose for a few seconds before raising on the balls of her feet, counting "one, two" to herself before she thrust her right leg to the side, toes pointed outward. Her nightgowned hampered her extension but she managed to perform a few of the complicated toe-tapping steps and crisscrossing maneuvers of the dance until she stopped, breathless, right toe forward and right hand above her head.

"Did I do good, Grandma? Maisy taught me how to dance the Fling."

"That was wonderful, Maggie!" The grandmother and her nurse clapped their hands enthusiastically.

"You scamps!" A teenage girl scrambled up the steps, laughing as she gathered her skirts. The bagpipes droned to silence, and applause followed. Short of breath, she reached the top steps. "I'm so sorry, Mrs. Lawrence, I promised them I would bring them up to say goodnight, but they didn't wait for me."

"Margaret performed the Highland Fling for us. She was delightful."

"She loves to dance. Now, come along, children, kiss your grandmama and say goodnight. You should have been in bed already. I will be fired as your temporary nanny."

"One more song and then I will retire for the night myself." The grandmother blew kisses.

The children giggled and noisily followed Maisy's instructions before trooping down the stairs. Maisy kissed the older woman's brow, waved to the nurse, and dashed after the children.

The music faded again, and the grandmother sighed. She glanced over her shoulder and nodded. "I think it is time for me to return to my room, Nurse Brock. I am weary just sitting here. But had I not suffered this nasty break to my leg, I would be down there kicking my heels with the best of them."

The nurse laughed and eased the wheelchair toward the bedroom door. "I have no doubt of that, Mrs. Wyatt. I have never met anyone quite like you."

"Is that a nice way of saying someone my age?"

"Well, there is that too, but you know that is not what I mean. Now let us get settled in your room. Your dinner will be coming soon." The nurse wheeled her into one of the bedrooms as the strains of another lively tune broke out below.

From her floating perch above, Terry frowned. She could not figure out the reason for the scene that had just played out below her. Although her common link to the family below would be Étienne and Clothiste, she was not in Margaret's lineage as Kirby was.

She had been the last to enter the portal. She wondered where Kirby, Stephanie, and Mary Jo were. Were they safe and waiting for her to return?

Perhaps there is a connection to Margaret's disappearance here. A quick sweep of her gaze around the room revealed no clues.

Knocking sounds drew her attention to the bedroom the grandmother and nurse had entered. Terry glanced down. A maid bore a tray in one arm and rapped her knuckles on the door with her free hand.

The music ended in the rooms below, but the boisterous conversation continued.

The door opened and the maid attempted to enter with the tray, but the nurse blocked her path. The nurse smirked and said, "Go back to the kitchens, you piece of trash. You don't belong here with decent folk." She grabbed the tray and closed the door abruptly.

The maid stood in place for a full minute, facing the door that had shut her out. She reached to her cap and tucked loose strands of hair under the ruffle before turning in a circle. She stepped toward the small table lined with bric-a-brac, picking up pieces and setting them back in place. The floor squeaked and she froze in place. With a furtive look over her shoulder, she walked toward one of the other doors and scooted inside. She picked up a lace shawl, running her fingers over the delicate fabric. Then she disappeared from view.

Terry waved her hands, trying to direct her body downward and closer to the door so that she could see what the maid was up to. After a few seconds of flailing her arms, she picked up a rhythm that seemed to overcome her weightlessness and her body shifted into an upright position before dropping slowly downward until her feet touched the floor.

She reached the doorway in time to see the servant girl empty the contents of a small brass jewelry box into the folds of her apron, replace the lid. Terry could not see her next move until the maid turned and bolted from the room head down. Terry thrust her hands forward to grab the woman, but her hands passed right through her.

When the woman raised her head to look around, Terry got the first close full-in-the-face look at the maid and stared in shock.

The woman in the act of stealing the jewels was Liana.

CHAPTER 11

Modern Day Portsmouth, Virginia

Becky Cramin, office manager and paralegal for the law firm of Dunbar and Cross, closed the door of their office building and shivered. She had not put on her coat since she was only running next door to Clothiste's Inn and instantly regretted her choice. She scooted down the sidewalk and up the steps to the back door of the B&B.

It took several minutes before Sandi answered the knock. She came to the door with red-rimmed eyes, holding a tissue to her nose. She gave Becky a weak smile. Since Norrie's disappearance, she had worked remotely from the B&B, but no one had explained the full reason to Becky.

Becky asked, "Is everything okay, Sandi?"

Sandi nodded. *What am I going to say—that I can't come in to the office because my child is lost somewhere in time?*

"It is, Becky." She managed another smile.

"Is Kirby here?" Becky held up a yellowed envelope. "A truly delicious-looking doctor that works with Kirby dropped this off for him a little while ago. I tried to call you, but your phone went to voice mail. I brought it over as soon as I had a free moment. Is Terry here?"

Sandi shook her head. *How to explain that those two were also lost somewhere in time?*

"They-they are both out for the moment. I can take the envelope and give it to Kirby when he-uh, when he gets back. Is there a message for Terry?"

"Her phone is going to voice mail too. Her ten o'clock called to reschedule and she's free for the rest of the day afternoon." Becky peered closer. "Did y'all party too hardy last night? Phones not charged, not checking in."

"No partying but we have been working on a—case that we just got. We'll fill you in on the details when we can." *Or as soon as we can come with a more plausible story than time traveling escapades.*

"Well, okay. Not to be rude, but it's too cold to stand here chatting." Becky backed down the steps, a concerned expression on her face as she looked at Sandi. "Are you sure you're okay?"

"I am." Sandi nodded and sighed. "I don't mean for it to seem like we are playing games but we really do have a serious matter we've been dealing with. Now go get your coat on before you come out again."

Becky gave a short wave. "You know where to find me if you need me. Y'all get those phones turned on in case I need you."

"Thank you, Becky." Sandi closed the door against the cold air. She glanced at the yellowed envelope with Kirby's name written in faded ink and set it on the counter. She grabbed the coffee pot and emptied the used filter pack. She replaced it with a fresh pack, filled the pot with water, and emptied it into the reservoir of the coffee maker.

As the fresh brew filled the air, she leaned her head in her hands and began a new round of tears.

Stephanie
Somewhere in Time

Stephanie floated along the dimly-tunnel. The only real illumination emanated from a rectangular shape at the far end of the passageway. Gentle breezes brushed past her face propelling her forward. The air warmed as she drifted nearer to the light. She glanced at the old doll in her hand. Despite the calm and not unpleasant atmosphere, melancholy shrouded her.

"Stephanie?" Distant voices called to her. She saw blurred images appear in the frame of light.

Suddenly her body thrust forward as if a turbo-booster had been turned on. The rectangular light enlarged as she flew closer to it. She held one hand in front of her in a protective pose. Unseen forces on the other side of the light clamped down on her wrist and pulled. She sailed through the lighted square as if passing through a glassless window.

She crashed into a solid object before both she and the object fell prone on the floor.

"Gage!" Stephanie had been pulled into the arms of her fiancé. He wrapped her in a tight hug. Beside Gage, Kyle lay on his back, one hand still clutching Stephanie's left wrist. Sandi stood nearby.

"What happened?" Stephanie cried, even as she smothered Gage with a kiss.

Before anyone could answer, the lights dimmed and hummed with electricity. Knickknacks rattled on tables and shelves, pictures clacked against the walls, pages of magazines flipped from cover to back.

"Someone else is coming!" The shout came from Chase, standing at the fireplace and staring at a strange glow in the mirror above the mantle. The glass quivered and a hand shot through.

Chase recognized the engagement ring and shouted, "It's Mary Jo!" He tugged but could not pull the rest of her body through. Sandi scrambled beside him and placed her hands over his. They tugged for several moments until Mary Jo's other hand reached through the undulating vermeil mirror.

Sandi grabbed that arm and readied her stance. Together she and Chase pulled until Mary Jo's head and shoulders emerged. Then she popped the rest of the way through like a champagne cork from a bottle. The chaotic movement around the room stopped as abruptly as it began, and the room settled into quiet. By then, Gage had scrambled to a standing position and pulled Stephanie to her feet, then Kyle. Everyone began to talk at one time.

"Mary Jo! Thank God." Chase folded her into his arms. "Are you okay?"

"Did you see Norrie?" Sandi pressed her hands to her stomach, her gaze flickering between Mary Jo and the now-normal mirror.

"Where's Terry—and Kirby?" Gage spoke next.

"Wait, everybody. One at a time, please, or we'll never figure out what's going on." Kyle's sensible voice calmed the small group.

Mary Jo shook her head. "I didn't see any of the others. I mean of our time period."

"Nor I," Stephanie interjected. "Where did you go, Mary Jo?"

"The battle at Yorktown, I think." Mary Jo shook her head. "I think it was the same place Kirby landed— maybe one of the last battles in the field. It was every bit like scenes of the old nightmares I've had since I was a child. I was like Molly Pitcher, helping load and shoot a cannon in a Yorktown battle. Where were you?"

"At some point very late in Nicole's life. She was an old woman and I was with her when she died. It was sad." Stephanie hugged the doll close to her heart.

"Listen, don't talk about it yet," Kyle suggested. "Get used to being home. Sandi and I will get some coffee—extra strong—and then you two can tell us what happened. Maybe we can find a clue to bring the others back,"

"Are you hungry?" Sandi asked.

"Starving, but I couldn't eat a thing," Stephanie glanced at the clock on the mantle. The hands were stuck just shy of the four o'clock position, and then she asked, "How did we get back here?"

"I don't know, but we knew you—or rather someone—was coming. Weird lights exploded from the mirror. Everything started going crazy and the clock spun. The hands whizzed backwards and then stopped, just like that," Chase said, pointing to the clock. "The only movement is the big hand straining to reach four o'clock. See how it quivers, like something is preventing it from making that last click?" He led the two travelers to the sofa, then glanced at his watch. "In reality it is nearly four-thirty."

"So, we've been gone about an hour and a half?" Stephanie studied the fluttering clock pointer. The arrow jumped back and forth, still unable to click into position. Then her eyes grew wide.

A green glow shimmered from the mirror. The candlesticks shook in place, an unlit log in the fireplace dislodged from the rack. Winds whipped around the room in a frenzy, blowing hair out of place and pushing pillows over the back of the sofa. Kyle and Sandi ran to the room, arms laden with trays as they braced against the forces blowing around them.

"Incoming!" Chase shouted as the house rocked on its foundation.

Norrie
Lost in Time

Norrie sat on the back stoop and wiped sweat from her brow. The day was getting hot.

Again.

She knew what would happen. It was the same thing every day.

The children played hide-and-seek. No one asked her name or where she came from. No one asked where her house was. No one, not even the twins Jack and Frank, asked her why she was there or why she had their sister's doll.

At first it was so much fun, to be around so many kids. But when the storm hit, they ran back to their homes and she just went—somewhere. She didn't know where she went, but the rains would come, the winds would whip up. And horrible thunder and lightning would crash around her.

Then she would be standing in the middle of the kids again as the hide-and-seek started.

The boy named Hank would cover his eyes and count down while the children ran to hiding places. Norrie would run to the magnolia tree and step inside the branches. It smelled like the fresh earth when she planted flowers with her mother. Sometimes it smelled like the basement of the library her mother took her to sometimes.

She stood just inside the limbs and peek out, watching as children ran by, laughing each time Hank found one of them.

She used to laugh with them but it wasn't fun anymore. No one ever found her and when the rains started, they just left her and ran home.

And they never found Margaret either. They called for Margaret. Sometimes the twins called for Maggie, or sometimes

"Maggot."

But no one ever asked her where Margaret was. Or why she had Margaret's doll.

It was all so strange. She played with all of the children, running and laughing as Hank called down his numbers, but they never seemed to find her.

This time when she ran to hide under the branches, she laid down and curled into a ball, holding Margaret's doll close to her.

Maybe she could pretend she was Alice in Wonderland and she was hiding in a rabbit hole.

"Mommy? I want to come home. Please, Mommy, come find me."

CHAPTER 12

Kirby's new travel
Somewhere in time

The dark chamber flashed with intermittent colored lights, which left streaks as they faded out. Margaret clutched her arms tighter around Kirby's neck and buried her head against his shoulder, muffling a scream. Kirby tightened his hold on the little girl, her hair lashing his face.

He noticed right away that something was different about this time travel. Although the winds still whipped by and sparkles brightened the darkness, his body was not subjected to the same painful twisting and pulling he had experienced in the past. Instead of whirling through a tunnel of opening and closing doors, he remained in one spot while scenes whizzed by.

Images of his past travel swept around him. Observing Étienne and Clothiste with the birth of their son Louis, later at various celebrations as their family grew. Louis the lost drummer boy, Louis the young boy selected by George Washington to infiltrate the British Army and spy for the American cause. Meeting Margaret by the clothesline. Trapped in the stinking prison. His escape to

Yorktown. As the battlefield scenes ripped past, he jumped with shock to see a modern-dressed Mary Jo holding position at the cannon with the colonial Marie Josephé, similar to an event he himself had experienced.

Laughter and the shouts of the children reached their ears and Margaret cried out. "I hear my brothers. Frank! Jack!"

"Olly olly oxen free!" Jack called. "Come on, Maggie, we have to go inside. You are safe to come out from hiding and you won't be 'it' next time."

"Papa's gonna give you a lickin' if you don't come in," shouted Frank. Both boys stood outside the branches of a wide magnolia tree. They leaned forward, hands on knees as they peered between sprawling limbs.

The wind whipped through the branches, turning many of the leaves upward. Ominous rumbles rolled closer. Voices grew louder as more children joined in the search, nearer ones calling from the backyard, others fading as the callers darted around the house.

"Frank, your mama said get inside right now," a girl shouted. Her voice softened when she added, "Where are you, Maggie honey? Please show yourself. A storm is coming."

Margaret wriggled. "I hear Maisy! She's Hank's big sister. She likes me and doesn't let the boys call me 'Maggot' or be mean to me. She taught me the Highland Fling. I'm home. I'm home." Margaret tried to break from Kirby's arms but he tightened his grip as a slow mist enveloped their feet and curled around his legs.

Maisy called again, her voice fading as she walked away.

A thunderclap crashed, so loud it had to be right overhead. A new wind rose. Kirby and Maggie spun forward, leaves and branches slapping their faces.

They landed side by side on a huge bough inside the tree. The foliage created a canopy, surrounding them in shadows. Kirby dangled precariously on the swaying limb. Before he could straighten, he fell backwards, crashing through smaller branches. He somersaulted and landed flat on his stomach, knocking the wind out of him.

Now this is the time travel that I have come to know so well. He rolled to a sitting position, and carefully flexed his arms. He looked up to see Margaret holding a small velvet pouch.

Thunder boomed, and lightning crackled, so close Kirby could swear electric currents tingled through his veins. Maggie jerked. The bag slipped from her hands and something metal fell out, hitting a branch below her. An emerald stone separated from the base and the two pieces landed in the brush. A gold timepiece tumbled after, hitting branch after branch. Her mouth gaped open as her horrified gaze followed the jewel pieces to the ground.

Huge droplets of rain slipped through the leaves, pelting her face as she scrambled down the trunk. Her foot slipped on the last limb and she fell backwards, knocking the wind out of her lungs.

Lightning slashed outside the boughs forming the tree cave. Inside, the gnarled branches took on grotesque shapes. Kirby scrambled to the little girl's side. Maggie's fingers wrapped around the watch and she stood on unsteady feet, Norrie's American Girl doll tucked under her arm. He scooped her into his arms and pushed his way through the foliage, twigs tearing at his shirt and entangling the doll Margaret still clutched close. Kirby tugged on the doll until it broke free from the spindly fingers of branches holding them back.

Thunder splintered the air and a lightning bolt seemed to crackle right outside the tree. Margaret shrieked in

Kirby's ear as he shouldered his way through the clutching limbs. He cleared the last limb with his left leg but his right lodged on a protruding root and he tumbled forward. He fell to the ground, doing his best to land on his side and shoulder to protect the little girl.

He clambered to his feet as torrential rains pounded their faces, blinding them. He froze at the sound of clomping horse hoofs. The rattle of an oncoming wagon joined the chaotic sounds of wind, thunder, and screaming child.

After a frenzied shout of, "Whoa!" the wagon came to a stop so close that Kirby's shirt buttons scraped the wood.

"Get in the back, man," the voice shouted. Mud squished underfoot as Kirby blindly felt along the sides until he came to the back. He plopped Margaret over the backboard and hauled himself behind her. The wagon lurched forward, and he tumbled the rest of the way inside. He and Margaret bounced with the jerky movements until the carriage slowed. As the driver eased up on the reins, a woman beside him screamed, "Don't stop!"

"We have to," he shouted.

"Keep going, Peter." The maid's voice took on a steely tone as she withdrew a small pistol from the folds of her skirt and pressed it to his forehead.

Peter's eyes widened and he raised his hand to grab the pistol.

Kirby crawled forward on his knees to face the driver. His hear thudded in his chest as he recognized the woman holding the gun.

Eerie green lightning crackled across the sky in time with the burst of thunder. The silhouettes of the man and woman took on skeletal shapes. A whirlwind raised the wagon into a spin.

When the twirling ended, the wooden cart dropped to the ground and spun once in the dirt.

The first woman, body returned to solid form, remained at the reins but beside her, the bench was empty.

Until from out of nowhere another woman crash-landed in the driver's seat in Peter's place. Seeing the gun pointing in her direction, Terry Dunbar instinctively swung a punch that smashed the woman's jaw and sent her into a boneless puddle on the floor.

The horses shied and Terry picked up the reins, gaining control of the wagon, nearly tumbling forward at the sudden lurch.

"What the hell just happened?" Terry looked around and her eyes bulged at the sight of Kirby and the little girl screaming behind him, her desperate cries fading to hiccupping whimpers as she raised her head.

"Oh, my God, Norrie! How did you get here? Kirby, is that you? Are you okay? You look like you have been through another battle at Yorktown. Are Stephanie and Mary Jo here?"

"No, I haven't seen them. Margaret and I—" He glanced at the little girl and a shocked expression formed on his face. "Norrie?"

Norrie burst into tears. In her hands she held a rustic doll.

"She has Margaret's doll!"

"What the hell just happened?" Kirby asked. "Last thing I remember is that Margaret and I were hurdling through time, and we landed in the center of the magnolia tree's branches. And Margaret still had Norrie's doll. There was a cloudburst and we got into a wagon, and then we got swept in a whirlwind. Now I am here in this wagon—but with Norrie and Margaret's doll?"

"I remember Margaret told us hands grabbed her into a wagon and everything spun around. She said that was how she came to be at a house where Abigail bought her as a servant. We must be reliving that moment."

"Yeah, I remember that. This must have been the point where Margaret first got lost in time, when I traveled back the first time and met her in seventeen eighty-one. Are we in the eighteen-hundreds or the nineteen-hundreds now?"

He hugged the frightened girl and she tightened her arms around his neck. "Are you okay, honey?

Norrie nodded, clinging to him. "I want my mother. I want to go home."

"We're going home, baby. She's waiting for you." He turned to Terry. "I have just been through some of the weirdest events of my life."

"Yeah, don't I know that. Kirby, I have seen so much in the last few…"

Kirby interrupted her, astonishment crossing his face. "Where did the man who was driving disappear to? That woman was holding him at gunpoint."

"Raise your hands where I can see them," a voice shouted. On either side of the wagon, two uniformed men approached. One carried a pistol, the other a shotgun.

Kirby, Terry, and even little Norrie did as commanded. The crumpled woman came to at that moment and sat up, looking around in a confused state.

Then she began screaming, "Officers, help me. Help me. These people are thieves and have kidnapped me and that child." The woman stood on unsteady feet and pointed her finger.

Kirby and Terry locked shocked stares into the

distorted face of an angry Liana. Before they could react, Liana screamed that the police could find a gun under the seat.

Terry and Kirby protested, each shouting over Liana to describe the scene they had just witnessed. A short, burly policeman blew on a whistle, causing Norrie to plug her fingers in her ears and wince.

"One at a time," the other patrolman, taller and skinnier, shouted. He pointed a long finger at Liana. "You first."

"Oh, officer," Liana sobbed. She held her hand out and the burly officer helped her from the wagon. She clutched his arm and buried her faced against his chest. "I am so happy you found us. It's been horrible, they have held me prisoner. They forced me to steal jewelry from a house in Portsmouth, and they were going to take me to a jeweler in Richmond to sell them. They grabbed the little girl there and planned to sell her to the gypsies."

"Oh, for Pete's sake!" Terry exclaimed, rolling her eyes skyward.

"Silence," commanded the skinny officer.

Liana outstretched her hand toward the more muscular of the pair and let her knees buckle in a melodramatic swoon. The officer gripped her around the waist.

She crooned, "I'm so grateful for your bravery. Oh, you are so strong." She flipped her hair back and batted her eyelashes.

"Oh, brother," Terry muttered. "And the Oscar goes to…"

The skinny officer pointed a gnarled finger at her and glared. "I told you to be quiet. Not another word. We're taking you all to the station and we shall get to the bottom of this there."

"Oh, please, Officer. I've done nothing wrong. It's these two who have been up to no good." Liana cowered and clutched again at the burly man's jacket. "I believe they have all those jewels taken from the Wyatt house."

"Well, we did have a report from Mr. Wyatt that some of his guests had been robbed." He patted her hand. "Don't you worry, little missy, we'll get it straight and have you on your way home in no time."

"Thank you, kind sir." Liana rested her forehead on his shoulder and shifted her face just a little to glance in Terry and Kirby's direction with a smirk.

"You are making a mistake, Laurel and Hardy," Terry began as she stepped down from the wagon and faced the tall, gawky fellow and his shorter, rotund partner. "I'm an attorney and..."

"Bah. A woman attorney? I have never heard of the likes. My name is Officer Stanley, and this is my partner Officer Oliver."

Terry bit back a laugh that the officers not only resembled the old slapstick comedy team but had last names that were the first names of the men. "If you search that woman's pockets, I'm sure you will find stolen jewelry. As I said, I am an attorney and..."

The tall skinny one who resembled Stan Laurel took in Terry's attire. "What are you wearing?"

Terry glanced down, then around. Her jeans and sweatshirt were not exactly *de rigueur* in—*what the hell century am I in now*?

"My friend is a playwright." She said with a nod toward Kirby. "He has designed costumes for a special play we are performing and today we were at a dress rehearsal."

Kirby raised one eyebrow and Terry gave an almost imperceptible lift of her shoulder before she directed her attention back to the officer. "And I am indeed an attorney and shall be prepared to have my law firm fight this to the fullest extent of the law."

"We don't have any charges, Stanley," Oliver Hardy's twin said with uncertainty. He turned to Liana. "Missy, do you have any jewelry?"

"I do, but they forced me to steal them. They held me at gunpoint. Look there, you will see the gun where she dropped it." Liana pointed to the wagon.

The lanky officer named Stanley peered into the wagon and lifted the gun from the floor.

"Check her for the jewels," Terry suggested. "If we forced her to take them for us, why would she still have them? Wouldn't we have taken them from her?"

Uncertainty crossed Stanley's face as he looked toward his partner.

He pointed to Norrie. "We are also looking for a missing little girl. Are you Margaret Lawrence?"

"My name is Norrie Cross. I'm not kidnapped-ed. I'm with my friends." She scrambled from the side of the cart and placed one hand in Kirby's and the other in Terry's, the doll tucked under her arm.

"What kind of clothes are you wearing?" The officer narrowed his eyes at the colonial dress Norrie had been wearing when she became lost in time.

"I am in his play." She inclined her head at Kirby, who exchange a sideward glance with Terry. She gave the little's girl's hand a gentle squeeze.

"Yeah, well." The police officer scratched his head and cleared his throat with a raspy "Harrumph." Then he added, "We will take all of you to the station with us now. Whose wagon is this?"

Kirby and Terry glanced at each other, neither able to provide an answer.

Liana nodded. "It belongs to Peter. Where is he? Does anybody know where he went? He was beside me, and then we found the little girl in the storm. The wind picked up our wagon. She and I landed in Richmond...but then we were back in the wagon...but this time Kirby got in with a different girl...but where is Peter?" Liana's voice trailed off as she looked around, fear and confusion etched on her face.

"We know nothing of that," Kirby said, shaking his head. "We were caught in the rain and the driver picked us up and..."

Liana shook her head and placed her fingers to her temples, her breath ragged as she strained with concentration. "No, it wasn't this child. Something is wrong. But where is Peter?"

"Enough. Get in, all of you." Officer Stanley gave an impatient motion to the back of the wagon as he helped Liana into the front seat and clambered beside her.

His burly partner lifted Norrie in the wagon. Terry shrugged off his arm and scrambled over the back. Kirby followed. The officer walked to the front and climbed into the seat. Liana slipped her hand through the crook of his arm, pressing her breast against him. The wagon rocked as the driver moved it forward.

"If I could get my hands on her, I could kill her," Kirby said.

"You want me to do it for you?" Terry started to crawl forward and Kirby pulled her back.

"Easy, tiger," he said. "We've got a mess to get out of as it is, we don't need a murder rap to boot."

"It won't be murder, it'll be justifiable homicide—maybe." Terry blew out her breath and settled back down. She wrapped her arms around Norrie's shoulders. "I'm glad these officers are not up-to-date on modern police procedures. If they had frisked us, they would have found my driver's license. How to explain that? By the way, Kirby, pull your shirt sleeve down and cover your watch so we don't have to explain light emitting diodes. What time is it, anyway?"

"I don't know. My watch stopped at three. I have a pocketful of coins that would have been impossible to explain. But that playwright quip to explain our unusual dress was brilliant." Kirby tugged his cuff over his watchband.

"Well, it worked. And that was very fast-thinking on your part, Norrie, to say you were in the play too, to explain your clothes." Terry hugged the little girl. "Are you really okay, Norrie baby? Your mama is fine, but she is so worried about you."

"I kept wanting to come home, Aunt Terry." Although she and Terry were not related, she had grown up with Tanner and had mimicked her little friend in calling her "Aunt Terry."

"What happened to you? You were with us when we left with your mama, remember, when we stood in line and watched the soldiers?" Kirby said gently.

Norrie nodded, then shrugged. "I twirled and twirled in the wind, Kirby. And when I stopped, I was near a big tree. I've been playing hide and seek with the other kids. There were the twins, Frank and Jack, and Hank and some others. Every day, we just play hide and seek. I hide from them, and then the same thing starts all over again. It's not fun anymore and I want to go home, Kirby. Please take me to my mama."

"I will, honey. You stay close to Terry. Things may happen soon."

Norrie nodded and scooted closer. They rode in silence.

Moments after the wagon stopped in front of the police station and they entered the building. Two small holding cells stood to the left of the room. Caged with iron bars, the spaces looked to be about four-square feet. Each had one narrow wooden bench running along the back against the wall.

Officer Stanley directed his partner to place Kirby in one cell while he ushered the three females into the other.

Terry and Norrie entered without a word, but Liana protested and tried to avoid passing through the door.

Chaos began anew in the sparsely furnished room.

"Why do I have to go in there? They are the criminals! Look at her necklace, look at his ring. I know they are stolen from the guests."

"Until we get this sorted out, everyone stays locked up," Officer Stanley ordered.

Liana flounced past the officer and plopped on the bench. The metal doors clanked shut. The police officer turned the key on the women's cell door, then locked Kirby in the one to the right.

"Kirby!" Liana dashed to the iron bars that separated the two prisoner enclosures. "Please talk to me."

Kirby faced her with such a cold hard stare that even Terry winced. She helped Norrie to the bench and sat as far away from the couple as four feet allowed.

"Who are you, Liana? I mean, who are you really"

"She's a thief, I can tell you that," Terry could not resist interjecting.

"How dare you?" Liana whirled on one foot.

Terry turned her own version of a cold hard stare at Liana, and then on a hunch repeated every movement she had witnessed when the maid stole the jewels.

Liana's eyes widened. "How did you know that?"

Terry ignored her and turned her face to the blank

141

wall.

"Kirby, Kirby. Wait, wait." Liana reached her hand through. Kirby stood with arms crossed, feet planted apart, just outside of Liana's reach.

"Kirby, listen. My name really was CarlyAnna Chambers. I was poor, spending my days waiting on rich people and never getting anywhere. Then something strange happened to me. I was in the carriage, much like we were today, and something odd happened. We spun and twisted through this horrible wind, and when everything cleared, I was on this street in front of a jewelry shop. It had been in operation in my time, and now I stood in front of it with a pocketful of jewelry, and surrounded by all these strange moving horseless carriages, and electric lights and a whole new world. I adapted quickly. No one ever realized I was a time traveler—well, at least that I came from another century. I never went to any other time period, just your century. The jeweler hired me, and I learned how to live in your time. I'm a fast learner, and I convinced him I was dressed like I was because I was in a play." She turned a contemptuous look on Terry. "Like *she* just did."

"I have one question for you, Liana. Was there ever a baby? Because so help me, if you aborted my child, I will kill you."

"I can do that for you here," Terry called over her shoulder. Neither Kirby nor Liana turned in her direction but remained locked in a staring standoff.

"No, Kirby. I am a lot of wicked things, but I am not a monster that would kill her own child. There never was a pregnancy. Just like Peter. You men are so stupid. It's so easy to trick you. I lied to him about the baby because I needed him to help me escape. I lied to you about the baby, because I wanted you back. Please forgive me."

Kirby turned on his heel and sat down, his back to her.

Hours ticked past. Norrie curled onto the narrow bench, resting her head on Terry's lap.

New commotion arose as two men and a woman entered. The man carried a disheveled young girl in his arms and rushed to the desk where Officer Stanley wrote in a ledger.

"Officer, I am Frank Wyatt, and this is my wife Celestine. This is her cousin, Daniel Lawrence. We had the robbery at our house last night, and then we reported Mr. Lawrence's daughter missing today. We are happy to report that after hours of searching, we found Margaret safely. She had fallen asleep in the branches of the old magnolia tree and no one could see her. She was wandering in the rain but none the worse for the wear-and-tear—except for our nerves. My wife was so distraught we had to call a doctor."

"But, Papa," protested Margaret. "I told you, I went away and was gone for ever so long. That mean lady kidnapped-ed me but my friends helped me get away, and then I saw President Washington—and then I saw the talking boxes and moving pictures and…"

"Quite an imagination there." Officer Stanley smiled.

Celestine Wyatt unfolded a lace fan and fluttered it through the humid air. "I am afraid I too-quickly dispatched a letter to my cousin Emily about Margaret's disappearance that will cause such a worry. I must send an immediate message to put her mind at ease."

"I am glad that your daughter is safe, Mr. Lawrence." The officer spread a cloth on a desk and shook the contents of the small pouch recovered from the wagon. "I was about to match these jewels to your report. I believe these were stolen from some of your guests?"

"Oh, you have found them." Celestine clasped her

143

hand to her heart. She rushed to the collection.

Margaret burst into tears. "Papa, I broked your ring. It's under the tree."

"I know, honey. I found it when I was looking for you. We will get it fixed."

"I don't know where Mama's watch is. I had it but now it's lost-ed." She cried harder, burying her head against his shoulder. She muffled,

"Don't cry, Margaret," Norrie called from her cell. "I have your doll here."

"Norrie!" Margaret screamed, startling the adults. She squirmed from her father's arms and rushed to the bars before he could catch her.

All heads in the room turned to the jail cells.

"Margaret!" The two girls slipped their arms around the bars and hugged.

"Harrumph." Officer Stanley scrubbed his hands over his face, then pulled a watch fob from his pocket. "It's nearly four o'clock. Let's get this finished so we can get out of here."

"That woman!" Celestine raised her hand and pointed at Liana. "That woman was my housemaid. She is the one who stole the jewels."

"She took your jewels!" Liana stood up and shouted, grabbing Terry and forcing her forward. "And she has your cross, Mrs. Wyatt, and he is wearing Mr. Lawrence's ring! I saw both of you with those pieces."

While Liana pushed Terry closer to the iron barriers, Kirby came face-to-face with his third great-grandfather. Daniel Lawrence looked him in the eye and then squinted at the ring Kirby wore.

Terry's face pressed against the bars as she met the astonished gaze of her own ancestress. The cross around her neck hummed and turned warm. She slipped her fingers over the gold cross. As Celestine Wyatt walked toward the holding pen, she mirrored the movement at her own throat.

Around her neck she wore the same gold pendant that Terry wore, a cross with a sapphire at the apex. The only difference was that Celestine's had been altered. Three rings circled the top of her cross, rings that had changed the shape from an ordinary cross to a Celtic cross. Back in her own century, Terry had a jeweler remove the rings to restore the cross to the original design Theresé had received.

Thunder rolled in and darkened the already gloomy office as two generations met.

Only a century and a half of time separated them.

Somewhere outside of the cinderblock police station, a church bell began to toll the hour.

As lightning crackled across the sky, the two little girls traded their dolls once more.

Norrie's doll Abby fell back into her rightful owner's arms at just the right moment in time.

CHAPTER 13

Modern Day Portsmouth, Virginia

"Incoming!" Chase repeated as he braced himself in front of the fireplace. The little hand of the clock remained steadily pointed to 4, but the hand of the clock jerked frantically toward the 12 position.

"I hear Norrie calling me." Sandi pushed Chase aside and gripped the mantle as furious winds whipped around them. "Norrie is calling me. Where are you, baby? I'm here."

Norrie's infectious giggle tinkled from the chasm behind the mirror as colorful sparkles swirled past them.

"Mommy! Where are you?" Her voice warbled, a tinny echo repeating her words.

"Keep coming to my voice, honey," Sandi shouted. She tried to push through the undulating surface, but her hands were blocked.

"Stop!" Kyle rushed forward and pulled her back. He pointed to the mirror. The greenish light pulsed and sparkles filled the interior of the looking glass.

Kyle tapped at the mirror closest to the frame. At least one inch of solid mirror rimmed the undulating surface, separating it from the gilt frame.

"Something is happening. When the strange occurrences began at this mirror, the whole thing, frame included, shimmered and quaked. Now, the frame is solid and this area closest to it has returned to mirror." He ran his fingers across the rippling façade, then brushed his fingers across the blurring image. The quivering dispersed in a trail behind his movement until his finger reached the other edge of the solid glass.

He turned to his friends, sure their hearts thumped as hard as his.

"The portal is closing. If we don't get them home, they may never get out of there." As he spoke, a small object shot through the glass and landed on the floor a few feet away.

Norrie's doll had returned to the 21st century.

"Norrie!" Sandi screamed, pounding on the mirror frame.

"Mommy! Mommy, where are you?" greeted her cries.

Kirby and Terry
Portsmouth, 1861

Liana's latest accusation caused another stir in the small police office, as Terry and Kirby raised their voices in denial of the charges. Officer Stanley blew on his whistle to no avail.

The burly policeman named Oliver returned with two men and a woman. One man carried a black medicine bag. He nodded to Officer Stanley and without a word took a seat near the desk. The second man, wearing a white shirt, stood by the door with his back to the wall and his arms crossed. The woman, dressed in a gray pin-striped dress with a white pinafore, took a position immediately beside him, a black-and-white checkered cloth folded over her arms.

Officer Stanley blew the whistle again and the room turned silent. He turned to Celestine. "Madame, may I ask you to verify if this woman has your necklace? And, Mr. Lawrence, is that your ring the gentleman is wearing?"

Daniel stepped closer and peered at the ring Kirby wore. "I must say that this emerald ring is very much like the one that has been in my family for generations, but it is not mine." He reached into his pocket and pulled out the frame of a man's gold ring. A prong was slightly bent, and although the base of the ring was different from Kirby's, the space where a stone had once rested looked to be the same size.

"Our daughter took my wife's watch and my ring to play with," Daniel continued as he held the band up. "We found the band while looking for her, but not the gem itself." He placed the ring back in his pocket. "We have yet to find my wife's pearl watch."

Celestine tapped her finger to her neck. "This woman did not steal my necklace. As you can see, I am wearing mine, and she hers. Though they are quite similar, mine is a Celtic cross and this woman's is a regular cross." She looked at Terry. "Do I know you?"

Terry said, "We have never met but we know many of the same people."

Celestine nodded to Terry, then pointed to Liana. "That woman, however, was employed as a servant in my home. Her name is CarlyAnna Chambers. During the party, she was known to be in the vicinity of the missing jewels after she took a tray of food upstairs. She never returned to the kitchen after that duty, and then we discovered the theft when our guests returned to their room."

"It wasn't me." Liana raced to the bars and motioned

wildly for her ally, Officer Oliver. "You must check these two out. They kidnapped me and forced me to steal the jewels. They come from the future. I was there myself, for many years."

"What is this nonsense?" Officer Stanley shouted. He glanced at the man with the medical kit, who nodded imperceptibly.

"It's true. I went to the future and lived there for many years. This man was at one time my fiancé. Tell them, Kirby."

Kirby shrugged. "I have no idea who this woman really is," he said simply.

"You bastard!" Liana screeched and charged over to the bars, trying to reach through to grab Kirby. "Tell them! Tell them about the carriages with wings that fly around the world."

She raced back to the front of her cell and shouted to the policemen. "They are called airplanes and can carry people across the oceans and faraway lands. In the future, people have big boxes in their homes from which they can watch moving pictures like plays and shows. They have little tiny boxes they can hold in their hands—" Liana motioned with her palm to show the size. "They can talk into these devices. They can see pictures of their loved ones and hear their voices no matter where they are in the world."

The doctor scribbled in a ledger and murmured to the officers.

"Tell them, Terry," Liana turned on her and shrieked. "Tell them how banks have machines in the wall and people can insert a plastic card to take out money."

"Machines that give out money? And what is plastic?" Oliver asked, turning to Terry.

Terry dismissed the question with a shrug.

149

Liana sputtered in frustration and stamped her foot. "Tell them about the other things in the twenty-first century. People ride in horseless carriages that can travel five or even ten times faster than a horse can run. And electric machines that wash clothes and dishes. And…"

"What is this ridiculous talk, woman?" Officer Stanley rose from his seat at the desk, and the doctor touched his arm. Stanley sat down.

"It's true." Liana ran her hands through her already-disheveled hair. Spittle shined on her chin and she swiped the back of one wrist across her mouth. "I lived in the future with them. But I took the jewels and hid. I made Peter come get me. Where is Peter?"

She looked around, eyes wild. "I took the jewels and he was taking me away in the wagon. I lied to him about the baby, but he said he would take me to Richmond if I stayed out of his life. We were riding in the alley and the storm came out of nowhere. We twirled in the air and I landed in the future. I have a boutique and buy and sell jewelry and antiques. I always wanted to have pretty things like other people had. I didn't want to be poor."

The room grew silent as all eyes stared. Even the little girls stopped playing with their dolls and turned to look at Liana with wide eyes.

The man with the medicine bag walked to Liana. A low, deep rumble of thunder rolled in the distance.

"Do you know who I am, Miss Chambers?"

"No." Lina shook her head frantically and backed away.

"I think you do," he said in a kind tone. "I am Dr. Foster."

"Yes, I know you now." Liana backed into the corner of the cell. "You sent me away. You sent me to the lunatic asylum. I won't go back there."

"You need help, Miss Chambers," Dr. Foster said. "You took things from your sister and you tried to hurt her. She almost died. We want to help you so you don't do that again."

"No! I won't go back." Liana lunged forward and grabbed Norrie around the neck, picking the child up from the floor and shaking her like a rag doll.

Terry jumped at Liana and tried to pull her hands away. Norrie gurgled, her eyes bulging. Margaret screamed from outside the cage and her father scooped her in his arms.

Officer Oliver grabbed the ring of cell keys, nervous hands shaking as he tried to open the door. He dropped the ring twice before he could insert the correct key and get inside the cell. Terry pulled Norrie free and kicked the back of Liana's knees until the woman's legs buckled. Then Terry leapt over the slumped form and exited the cell with Norrie in her arms.

The nurse in gray and her companion rushed inside. The nurse unfolded what looked like a lady's blouse but with six-foot-long sleeves. Liana struggled and lashed at them. The doctor entered the tight space with a hypodermic syringe in one hand. He aspirated the needle, then injected the medicine into her arm. After a few seconds she stopped thrashing and sank to a sitting position, awake but calm. The attendants pushed her arms into the sleeves, swathed the loose ends around her body and then secured them in the back. The male lifted Liana by one elbow while the nurse took the other. They half-carried, half-dragged the semi-conscious woman from the cell.

Dr. Foster held the front door open and remained behind after the staff left. He swiveled on his heel and pulled a handkerchief from his pocket to polish his spectacles.

"Miss Chambers is a very sick woman. Her family had her committed to the Eastern Lunatic Asylum in Williamsburg two years ago, after she nearly killed her younger sister in a jealous rage. The doctors thought she was getting better and allowed her to come home for a day visit. She disappeared during the family outing and no one knew where she went or what happened to her. As happens, when missing persons are not immediately found, the search grows cold. Fortunately, Officer Oliver recognized her picture from the drawing."

Stanley walked over to a bulletin board and removed a yellowed wanted poster. He turned around and held up an artist's rendition of a woman's face—Liana's.

He grinned. "Oliver's not as dumb as he looks." He sat back down and shuffled papers. "Now—let's get this sorted out so all of you good people can get back where you belong."

A clap of thundered clashed with the first toll of the church bell and Kirby shouted to Terry, "Grab hold of Norrie!"

Terry reached for the little girl, scooping her up just as winds sucked them into their twirling vortex. They shot forward in a burst of light, hurtling like a missile through space down a tunnel awash with an ever-changing kaleidoscope of colors.

A cacophony of noises assaulted their ears. Bells clanged incessantly, hammers pinged against brick, doors opened and slammed shut. Laughter, crying, shouting.

The rush of cascading rain overtook the roar of cannon fire.

Norrie's whimpers muffled as she tucked her face into Terry's shoulder. Terry tightened her grip. Through the abyss they twirled. Bagpipes droned, car horns honked, horse hooves clattered on cobblestone, all competing with the other clatter to be the prominent auditory in the chaotic visual.

At the long end of the tunnel, the small rectangle glowed and seemed to beckon them. Terry grimaced as the rushing winds brought tears to her eyes, but her hear skipped a beat at the realization that the opening appeared to get smaller as they got closer.

"Norrie!" Sandi's voice filtered past, seeming to break up around them.

"Terry." Kyle's voice reached Terry's ears in a low, slow-motion shout.

"Mommy!" Norrie tried to raise her head, but the forces prevented movement.

"Kyle! We're coming!" Terry fought against the winds to stretch one hand ahead of her toward the light.

She reached through the narrowing shaft and hands grabbed her wrist, tugging her through what appeared to be a waterfall.

She broke through the shimmering barrier, coming face-to-face with Chase and Kyle, each of whom gripped her arm with both hands.

Then a pulling motion tugged her back into the abyss.

CHAPTER 14

One of Terry's arms dangled through the mirror as her body slipped back through the portal. Kyle managed to move his hand to her elbow as she melded back into the mirror.

The frenetic hands of the clock burst from their holding pattern, and the clock tolled the first strike of five.

"Pull harder, Chase!" At Kyles urging, Chase tightened his hands around Terry's wrist and heaved back. A third set of hands seized hold of Terry's sleeve, the only thing Gage could reach as he joined the fray, elbowing between Kyle and Chase.

A second clang sounded, echoing as Terry's head and one shoulder popped through again, then her other shoulder, Norrie tucked under her wing. The three men managed to get Terry's upper torso and all of Norrie into the room before the hardening mirror closed tighter.

The trio rocked back and forth. Kyle shouted, "On three!" He counted and on "three" the men heaved with all of their might.

The next clanking toll seemed to shake the foundation of the house. Terry dropped Norrie to her feet, but she herself was still hung up. Her lower legs still remained on the other side, but through the mirror she saw the hands draped around her calves. Kirby's emerald ring glowed with a radioactive green.

The fourth toll reverberated.

"One more time," she begged. The men repeated the movements and yanked.

Terry shot through the portal, Kirby behind her, holding on to her legs for dear life. The three rescuers and two time-travelers crashed into a heap, tangling with Norrie and Sandi as she reached for her child.

The discord in the room reached a crescendo amidst a boom of thunder outside and the roar of frenzied winds whipping inside the room. Furniture rose an inch from the ground and landed back in place with a crash.

The final bell tolled, and then clock arrows spun wildly until they stopped in place at five o'clock.

Deafening silence permeated the room.

Kyle was the first to get to his feet. He slapped the solid face of the mirror, then turned to the group. "I think if you had not gotten through that portal before that mantle clock had finished tolling five o'clock, you would have never made it back."

***

Each of the four travelers had shared their stories, comparing notes on the similarities or differences in their experiences, and speculating on the phenomena that had occurred.

"So…" Kirby drew the word out. He sat on one end of the sofa, a sleeping Norrie separating him from Sandi, who sat on the opposite end with her daughter's head on her knees. The little girl, none the worse for her adventures, snored softly.

Sandi had welcomed him home with a hug and thank you for bringing back her daughter, but tension still resonated between the couple. Kirby pulled the coverlet over Norrie's feet and patted them, then continued. "You are suggesting some of us witnessed some of the same events, but from a different perspective or with a slightly different outcome?"

Kyle nodded. "It's the only explanation I can offer. For whatever reason, the souls of your ancestors were locked in a time abyss, where all of those events that had happened to them were never fully resolved and had some kind of effect on their descendants."

"So, although it seems Kirby was on that same battlefield as I, he was there at a different time and for a different reason? Even though we both assisted Marie Theresé with the cannon, he was there to provide medical expertise that did not exist in that period, which influenced both Louis and Amable to become doctors. While Kirby may not have actually altered history by saving lives of someone who might have died, he would have provided medical care that made their later lives better."

Kyle half nodded, half shrugged.

"Ok, even if we go with that theory—and believe me, this is all so crazy that anything sounds sensible. Why did I go back to almost the same time and scenes?"

"Well, Mary Jo, you said you used to have those war dreams," Kyle said. "So, I think meeting Marie Josephé on the battlefield was meant to resolve your—" he waved his hands in search of the word.

"My issues?" Mary Jo said with a smile.

He nodded. "Okay. If you will—your issues—and Marie Josephé's as well. Meeting you again and wearing her necklace one last time perhaps released her from the final thing holding her here."

Chase asked, "So how could they…" He swept his hand toward Mary Jo and Kirby. "How could they each travel to that same place in Yorktown?"

"Chase, you know as much as I know. As much as any of us knows." Kyle scraped his hands through his hair. Little tufts stood up and Terry brushed them down with an affectionate touch.

He smiled and continued, "If there is any explanation, I would suggest it comes from the possibility that we are dealing with 'alternative histories' that exist side by side. It is a popular theme in fiction books, especially historical novels, in which one or more significant events occur differently. The author might approach some historical event with 'what if' suggestions at crucial points and present outcomes other than those recorded in history."

Chase scratched his head. "I don't know what else could explain this."

Kyle nodded in agreement. "From what you all learned in your time travels, Liana—CarlyAnna—was in a wagon making its way down the alley just at the time Margaret had run out from under the tree, and almost into the path of the wagon. This person Peter pulled her into the wagon. The next strike of lightning sent Margaret to the past, Liana to the future where she made a life for herself, and Peter went—where?"

"Dunno. But what about the watch and ring?" Chase persisted.

"Well, we know from Kirby's family history that Daniel eventually found the stone and had it remounted in a new setting, which Kirby eventually inherited in its present form. I'm just guessing, but both rings could exist at the same time because they were both in an altered state. Daniel only had the base of the ring when he came to the station, while Kirby had the new version of the ring."

"And at some point, my necklace had been altered to include circles around the stipes of the cross to make it appear Celtic, as the version Celestine wore," Terry added.

Kyle nodded. "And when you had those circles removed and returned the necklace to its original state, you wore a different cross than the one your ancestress wore. As for the watch, it somehow wound up with Liana in her twenty-first century capacity as a jewelry shop owner. We may never know how she found it or what had happened to it, but it was the catalyst that set things in motion."

"So, we each traveled to a different time that paralleled a real event from our ancestors' pasts and brought conclusions? But we didn't really alter history, did we?" Stephanie asked.

"I don't think so. All you were doing was settling the restless spirits of your ancestors. The jewels were returned to their original owners, even if only for a few minutes. It looks like everything is as it should be. All of the time travelers are back where they belong. The little girls are back in their respective centuries, as are their dolls."

At her last words, Sandi placed a protective arm over Norrie's shoulder. The little girl, curled beside her mother on the couch, shifted and turned, drawing her doll closer.

"Shall I be the one to address the elephant in the room?" Terry said.

"Don't do it, Terry," Stephanie warned in a low voice.

"No, no. Let's confront this head-on. We have to think about Liana. If she was a time traveler from the past, does that mean she never really existed in our time?

That she was never a shop owner, or jeweler, or whatever she was—or that we never really saw her, or that she and Kirby never met or…" Terry stopped short and looked at Kirby and Sandi. Sandi held her hand to her throat, while Kirby ran his hands through his hair.

"I-I'm sorry about all of this. But wherever she is, we know she can't escape," Terry said. "We'll just have to look tomorrow to see if there is any evidence she ever really existed in our time."

"This is all too freakin' unbelievable," Gage said. Standing before the picture window, he held Stephanie in a protective embrace. "You know we can't ever tell the rest of the family this story, don't you? Or anyone for that matter."

"Ha, no problem there," Terry said. "Sandi and I would be disbarred immediately."

"Wouldn't help my military career in the least," Kirby added.

"Although it could be good for my business," Mary Jo said. She waved her hands in an imaginary banner. "I can see the slogan now. 'Come to Clothiste's Haunted Inn. You never know where it will take you.'"

"Ooh, that's not even funny, Mary Jo." Stephanie sucked in a breath and shivered. "Do you think it will be safe for guests to stay here in the future?"

"I do," Mary Jo said firmly. "Can't you feel the peace? I've never, ever felt threatened in this place, but there's a quiet, a contentedness that I don't believe I have ever felt before. Can you feel it?"

The four couples paused. The tranquility enveloped them.

"It's starting to snow!" Stephanie pressed her nose closer to the glass and peered outside.

"And on that note, my love, it is time for us to get out

of here." Gage kissed Stephanie on the nose.

"And we have a wedding to plan." She draped her arms around his neck and nuzzled his jaw.

"Get a room," Terry said, rolling her eyes skyward.

"Pardon me, folks, but my bride-to-be and I are about to depart." Gage drew Stephanie toward the coat rack and held out her parka. "Don't panic if you don't see us for a few days. For the next forty-eight hours, I am going to know exactly where she will be and what she will be doing." Stephanie slipped her arm through one sleeve and Gage smothered her with a kiss.

"Don't start practicing now," Terry said as she shooed her brother and his fiancée out the door.

"And I have to get back on my new job at the new distillery," Chase said. "My crew said they found an old room behind a wall we are tearing down and I want to get over…"

Mary Jo put her finger under Chase's chin, turned his face toward hers, and kissed him full on the mouth, then said, "No shop talk. We are leaving now too." She grabbed his hand and led him toward the back of the house, calling over her shoulder, "Don't look for us for a few days either."

"I'll help you clean up, Terry." Sandi lifted Norrie's head and eased from the seat until she could stand up. She placed a pillow under her daughter's head and covered her with the afghan.

Terry tipped her head back and belted out a laugh. "Me clean up? Surely you jest, partner of mine. We shall leave this place as it is and I will call the cleaning crew in tomorrow for a thorough scrub down—and a nice bonus—to prepare this place for our first real guests this weekend."

"Well, I hope that you have a real innkeeper in place

by then. My temporary duties are more than fulfilled. I'm sure you will forgive me if I clear Norrie's and my things from the room and not return here for a long, long time."

"I'll help you," Terry said. "Kirby and Kyle will stay here to guard Norrie."

Kyle gave a thumbs up. "We've got it covered."

With a last glance back at her daughter, Sandi allowed Terry to draw her toward the hallway leading to the innkeeper's suite.

Sandi grabbed her small suitcase and scooped things in willy-nilly.

Terry went to the bathroom and packed toiletries in the little bag on the counter. She took Norrie's pint-sized pink bathrobe from a hook and a bottle of bubble-bath from the side of the tub. Satisfied she had all of Sandi's and Norrie's belongings, she took the items to the bedroom and placed them in the bag. Sandi made a sweep of the room, checking dresser drawers and the closet, then zipped the bag shut.

Terry cleared her throat. "Listen, I don't know what happened between you and Kirby, but I hope you give him a chance to fix things."

"Terry…" Sandi warned.

"Don't even get that tone of voice with me, sista." Terry turned Sandi to face the door and pushed her forward. "You two have been through too much together, in a short time. Fix it."

Sandi heaved a sigh and shook her head as she walked down the short hall.

Kirby stood when they entered the parlor. "I need to get my things from my room as well."

"We'll wait for you," Kyle said. "I think we should make sure everyone has left the building tonight. Tomorrow will be a new day for us all."

Kirby nodded and bounded up the staircase. He threw clothes in his duffle back, and gathered shaving items to throw in the kit. When he came down the stairs, Sandi was rousing a sleepy Norrie from the couch.

"Can I help you with your bags?" he asked.

"No, Kyle just took everything out for me." Sandi cleared her throat. "Um…look, I need to get Norrie in her own home, in her own bed. But I know we need to talk. Do you feel up to it?"

"Yes. Yes, I do." Kirby ran his hands through his tousled hair.

"Come over to my house in about an hour?"

"I'll be there." He turned out the hall lights and followed Sandi through the kitchen, turning the other lights off before closing the door to Clothiste's Inn.

Kyle had started the engine to Sandi's car, and she buckled her daughter in the back seat.

"Thank you, guys" she said as she turned to hug her friends. She slipped in behind the driver's seat and buckled in. She exited the parking lot with a little toot on her horn.

Kirby hugged Terry and shook Kyle's hand, then jumped into his own vehicle and drove away in the direction of his apartment.

Kyle and Terry waved from the sidewalk until both cars were gone.

"I hope they will be okay," Terry said.

"Me too." Kyle pulled Terry close to him. "I was never so scared as I was when we were waiting for you, and I was so afraid you were going to get stuck on the other side of that mirror."

"I was afraid I was going to be stuck half in and half out," Terry said with a laugh that changed into a shudder. "I am so glad all that is over with."

She kissed Kyle before taking his hand and leading up the steps to the apartment above the law office.

Peter McGowan
Somewhere in Time

Peter reached out and touched the cold dark walls.

He shook his head in confusion. He was back in the boundaries of that indefinable black hole. He'd long ago accepted that he was not dead, just stuck in a limbo from which he made periodic, unexpected escapes.

He'd experienced time travel before, popping in and out of strange locations and different years, but never to his own past.

Until now.

Somehow, he'd found CarlyAnna again, not in their time but in a new era. One moment they were standing in the parlor of that house, then the next they were swept away.

Through the mirror? *He and CarlyAnna twirled through lights, winds, and blurred objects until they landed in the very spot where he'd last seen her.*

Back to 1861 and the moment he and CarlyAnna raced away from Portsmouth, the wagon rattling through the narrow alley.

Then the storm hit, and the little girl ran into their path, screaming. Peter slowed and plucked her to safety.

Lightning crackled and thunder boomed. The winds lifted the wagon and when it landed, CarlyAnna and the little girl were gone. Police arrested him. He faced accusations of theft and kidnapping and was eventually sent to prison.

What just happened? *Peter's shouts echoed in his ears.*

He and CarlyAnna rode in the wagon again. He rescued the little girl again. CarlyAnna crammed a pistol to the child's head again.

Winds sucked the coach off the ground again.

This time when the spinning stopped, he was not alone in the wagon. He was not even in the wagon.

He was back in his dark, silent void, the only sound his own thumping heartbeat.

His limbo.

Or hell. Was he in hell?

He was never sure which. He would have brief reprieves from his torment, only to plunge again into the total darkness, with the pulse of his heart pounding in his ears and too much time to reflect on what had happened in his life.

He slipped his hand in to his pocket and frowned as he withdrew a ladies' brooch watch.

Where did this come from?

The dull thud of metal rocked his dark room and he tilted his head.

Was that a hammer against brick?

He squinted toward the small square of light that had beguiled him for years. He would run for it, chase after it, and yet—it always remained out of reach.

Something was different this time.

Piece by piece, the lighted space widened.

Where would he be this time?

And when?

CHAPTER 15

After a shower and shave, Kirby headed to Sandi's. He circled the block twice just to take in the sight of houses along her street ablaze in Christmas decorations. The snow had been short-lived, just enough to dust the lawns and add to the festive air.

The joy of the season did not ease his anxiety. A heaviness hung in his mind, with a dread dragging on his heart that he could not shake.

Had it only been last week that he and Sandi had taken Norrie to Busch Gardens for Christmas Town? They had returned from the excursion full of Yuletide cheer and new feelings.

The voice message left on his phone had been the first blow to his budding relationship with Sandi.

His failure to act on it immediately compounded the issue.

Then the hands of fate—and that damn mantle clock—propelled him into the fantastic journey back to the Revolutionary War. Gone only hours in reality, he had lived through weeks and months of life in colonial Portsmouth and other settings, met his ancestral family, and witnessed the British surrender at Yorktown.

And an 18th-century encounter with Sandi in a French army tent that had rocked his world for all time.

All-in-all, a fantastic journey—well, two fantastic journeys, considering he was just back from his second time travel— that could never be shared with any but a small group of people.

Kirby pulled into the driveway in front of Sandi's house. There was a single candle in a window but no other signs of Christmas.

Not that Sandi had even had a chance to decorate When Norrie failed to return to the 21st century, the distraught mother had only left Clothiste's Inn once.

Kirby flopped his head against the headrest. His stomached clutched as if a fist had rammed him.

Will I be able to salvage our relationship?

The front door opened, and Sandi stood silhouetted in light. He blew out his breath and cut the engine off.

His heart flipped. Could a candle in the window and a woman at the door be a good sign?

It can, can't it? With a sigh, Kirby exited the car and walked up the sidewalk.

"I was afraid you were going to sit out there all night," she said as she took his coat.

"I was afraid to come in," he admitted. "How is Norrie?"

"She's asleep. All the way home she kept talking about these fantastic dreams she had and now she wants to go to Yorktown. I told her maybe after the holidays."

"Kids are so resilient. Margaret didn't look a bit fazed about everything she had been through either."

"They do better than the adults. Coffee? I made a pot."

Kirby nodded, and glanced around the cozy living room. Gas logs burned in the fireplace, and several candles flickered on the tables. Pictures of varying sizes lined the walls and tabletops. He walked around the room to glance at photos. Most were of Sandi and Norrie at various ages, but several had group photos with Terry and other members of the Dunbar family, including several with Tanner.

He bent to peer at a photo on a side table. Tanner and Norrie stood together, arms draped around each other's shoulders. Tanner wore a colonial drummer boy costume and Norrie a long gown and bonnet.

"You have a nice place," Kirby called as he stood, nearly bumping into Sandi. She sidestepped and carried a tray to the coffee table.

"Before Terry and I became law partners, we worked at other offices. Our firms each had clients involved in a mutual case, and I guess no one thought it would amount to much, so it went to the junior lawyers. Terry had two clients and I had one. Together, she and I pulled off a coup so successful that we were able to leave our firms and open our law office. Terry put a down payment on her Maserati and I put one on this house."

She motioned for Kirby to sit on the couch. She sat down. Kirby noticed she sat closer, not hunched against the armrest.

Isn't that a good sign that she's not creating distance between us? Kirby's hand trembled as he reached for the coffee he really didn't want. *She could have sat in that chair across the room, right?* He returned the cup to the saucer.

"Sandi, I have to tell you how sorry I am…"

She held up a hand. "Kirby, please. There is no need to apologize for anything. We've been through a lot. Things were not normal."

He shook his head in disagreement. "That doesn't matter. I know you were badly hurt by Norrie's father. I didn't want to do the same. I wanted to tell you, and never found the right time. I owed you complete honesty, and I just hope that finding that message from Liana before I could tell you has not hurt our chances."

"That bitch." Sandi picked up her cup and then smacked it back in the saucer and turned confused eyes to Kirby. "But did she even exist? Was she ever real?"

Kirby heaved a sigh. "She was as real in our time as we were in hers. It is hard to believe that I spent the last few years of my life involved with a woman who apparently didn't even belong in my time. Or that she could have manipulated me so easily."

"Oh, she could be manipulative, I could see that even in the short time I knew her. If I could have knocked that bitch on her ass when I saw that text..." Sandi curled her hand into a fist. Kirby smiled and put his hand over hers. She did not pull away.

"I'm so sorry about that. It should never have happened like that. But the good news is there was never a baby, it was just a ruse to trap me."

"Still, I wouldn't have minded decking her once or twice."

Kirby laughed. "Terry landed a beaut. I had to pull her back from Liana a couple of times. You and she must make a formidable team in court. I'd hate to rile either of you."

"Terry is not someone to mess with when she's riled up." Sandi paused, her breathing more rapid. "Do you think she can come back? Liana, I mean?"

He shook his head. "I don't think so. Didn't Kyle say the portal was already closing on us as Terry, Norrie, and I were coming back?"

Sandi patted her heart. "Kirby, it was frightening to watch as it started to turn back into a solid mirror, that quivering cascade shrinking in size, and you three still on the other side. We somehow knew it would soon close forever. Then, I had visions of Terry and Norrie stuck halfway through, forever unable to move. I was afraid it could be like that movie *Jumanji*, where that kid was stuck between the floor and the ceiling."

"Truth is stranger than fiction. But maybe Kyle has it correct. What did he call it, alternate histories or something, in which one or more significant events occur, but differently? I guess that is what you could say happened in that movie. Didn't Kyle say that an author might approach some historical event with a 'what if' point of view at crucial points and present outcomes other than those recorded in history?"

"Like what if we put all of this behind us and move forward as if it never happened?" Sandi took his hand and rubbed her thumb across the knuckles. "What if we just start new?"

"Can you do that?"

"I put that candle in the window for you, Kirby. As long as we can see the light shining, we can do anything together." Sandi nodded and swallowed hard, her face straight ahead. "That sounded corny, didn't it?"

Kirby's heart nearly thumped put of his chest. "No, it was perfect. I've never known anyone like you, Sandi. I want you and Norrie to be part of my life for as long as I live." He moved closer and turned her chin until she faced him. The pulse in her neck danced and he touched his fingertips to feel it jump with the same frantic beat as his heart. She swallowed again before her eyes met his. He framed her face with his hands and brought his lips to within an inch of hers.

"As long as I can see the light in your eyes dance like that, I'll never need another candle in the window."

***

Holiday cheer was in full swing when Kirby arrived at the Dunbar family home for Christmas. He had covered the night shift at the hospital, and gone straight to Sandi's house, where he found mother and daughter with gifts unopened, waiting for him to share the occasion with them. After a light brunch, they had left him to catch some sleep before dinner with Terry's huge extended family.

He drove down the tree-lined drive and rounded the curve that brought the impressive restored farmhouse into view. He could not help but remember his Thanksgiving visit where he first learned he was indeed a member of the family, descended from Étienne and Clothiste's only son.

He wished his folks could have made it. They had come for a short visit two weeks earlier, where he introduced them to the Dunbar family and Sandi and Norrie, but they had to return unexpectedly so they could assist an elderly neighbor who had suffered a fire in his home. Then their Christmas Eve flight was canceled due to weather. He had tried to call all morning and kept getting voice mail.

He pulled into the yard and found a place to park near the dozen cars crowded along the drive. The front door opened, and two Irish setters bounded out, skidding across the front porch and down the steps, Norrie and Tanner close on their heels.

"Kirby, Kirby!" the kids shouted.

Norrie grabbed his hand. "Come on, we have a big surprise inside for you."

"Didn't I just see you a little while ago opening presents?"

"Did you know Santa brought us presents here, too? We've been waiting for you. Hurry inside so we can open them."

"Well. let's go, then." He scooped each of the kids in an arm and rushed up the steps. Giggles and barks accompanied him through the door as he maneuvered to avoid the dogs running between his legs. He wiped his feet on the Santa doormat, setting off a ringing rendition of "Jingle Bells" and a new round of dog barking.

"Kirby's here," Norrie shrieked. "Where's his surprise?"

"Settle down, young lady," her mother said with a laugh. Kirby set the two kids on their feet and she greeted him with a hug.

He nuzzled her ear and whispered, "I thought I had already unwrapped *everything*—under the tree and elsewhere."

"Stop it," she giggled. "People are watching." She turned Kirby around and he saw a gaggle of faces looking at them.

"Merry Christmas, everyone! It smells great in here. Joan, thank you for having me." Kirby reached to give the matriarch of the Dunbar family a hug. Over her shoulder, two more people moved forward.

"Mom, Dad?" Kirby stopped short. "What are you guys doing here? I thought your flight was canceled. I've been calling all morning to wish you Merry Christmas."

"We rented a car at the airport last night and drove straight here." Patrick Lawrence greeted his son with outstretched arms.

"All the way from New York?"

"Yep." Kirby's mother Rachel enveloped him in her arms. "Good to see you, son."

"Aw, man, this is a great surprise. How did you work

this out?" He clapped his father on the shoulder, then drew him in for a hug.

His mother said, "We were so disappointed our flight was cancelled, we checked the weather and saw that if we could get out of Newark, we'd be clear of the snow once we got to the other side of the Delaware Bridge. Between the weather and everyone else with the same idea, to took us almost six hours just to get to New Castle, so we got a room. Then we had more snow all the way to DC. We had hoped to get to your place when you got home from work, but since that wasn't going to work, Charles and Joan were gracious enough to let us surprise you here."

"This is such a great surprise." Kirby beamed, and hugged her.

"Okay, now can we open our other presents from Santa?" Tanner begged.

"Let Kirby say hello to everyone, honey," his mother Beth said. She put a hand over her baby bump. "Whew, this baby is kicking up a storm."

"Are you okay?" Connor, the youngest Dunbar sibling, rushed to his wife's side.

"I'm fine, honey." She smiled. "And we have a doctor here if we need him."

Kirby greeted the expectant parents before Sandi led him around the room to engage the huge gathering, most of whom he had met at Thanksgiving. First, he greeted the complicated family of Mary Jo, who had been raised by her single mother, only recently learning the identity of her father, as well as her relationship with Joan's cousin Hannah, the cantankerous baker at Mary Jo's French café.

Kirby hugged the diminutive woman and said, "I see your penchant for snarky sweaters doesn't disappoint us for Christmas."

With a wink, Hannah twirled. Green letters on the

front of her white shirt spelled out, "I'm on the naughty list and it was worth every minute." On the back, red letters said, "Yes, it was."

Stephanie rounded the kitchen counter and held her arms out to Kirby. "Kirby! Merry Christmas."

"You too, Stephanie. What are you cooking?"

"Me? Nothing. I'm only allowed to slice and dice, and maybe boil water for eggs or if we need to deliver a baby."

A puzzled look washed over Kirby's face until he realized Stephanie was joking about her well-known lack of cooking skills. He laughed and asked for Gage.

"On the deck with the other guys, watching his dad man the outdoor fryer, and probably taking bets on whether Dad or Chase will win the carving contest."

Thanksgiving had been Kirby's first opportunity to observe the friendly competition between the two men as they whittled their way through the roasted turkey, Charles the patriarch wielding a carving knife and Chase the contractor an electric knife.

"Well, my money's on Charles. He's pretty quick with that carving knife."

"They are talking of challenging your skills as a surgeon, so watch out."

"Maybe next year." Kirby winked and stepped outside to greet the small group gathered on the deck, where his own father and Mary Jo's had arrived before him. A few feet away, a deep fryer held the bubbling contents of the second turkey for the feast.

"You're just in time, Kirby," Gage greeted. "Five more minutes and this bird is cooked. Brewskis are in the cooler."

Kirby exchanged pleasantries and dug a beer from the cooler while the turkey reached the last stage of frying.

***

Joan Dunbar wiped tears from her eyes as she flipped through a book in her lap. The second round of gifts that "Santa" had brought to the Dunbar home had long been unwrapped. Newcomer Patrick Lawrence had been appointed as the official scorekeeper for the turkey carving contest, and he declared a tie. The family had enjoyed the bountiful feast, and now relaxed with coffee and pie while Tanner and Norrie sipped hot chocolate at their little table and chair set.

Then Kyle and Stephanie, the genealogy enthusiasts, presented Joan with her final gift.

"This is beautiful, Kyle and Stephanie. This family history book is one of the most precious gifts I have ever received. I thought that when you gave me the first part of this gift." She turned her gaze to a family tree poster filled with names. "But then to have the stories of all of these people put into one book is incredible."

Stephanie sat on the arm of Joan's chair and brushed her fingertips across the open page. "This is still a work in progress. There are many people we still need to research. We won't find every link, but it is fascinating to look for clues."

Kyle leaned against the opposite arm and patted his future mother-in-law's shoulder. "Your Wyatt line that traces back to Étienne and Clothiste is very well documented, which also helped us complete the connections for Stephanie, for Mary Jo and Hannah, and of course, for our newcomer, Kirby, through his father's line. You can even join the Daughters of the American Revolution. Celestine was a member."

"I just love this." Joan traced her fingers over names

in the book. "Why is this name by Étienne and Clothiste's children with an asterisk? A-m-a-b-l-e? How do you pronounce it? I've never heard it. Did they have another child?"

"Amable?" Kyle asked. "It is an archaic French name pronounced 'AM-a-bull' and means lovable. He was not a blood relative of the family, but an orphan they took in. Stephanie said that Clothiste mentions him a number of times in her journals."

Stephanie nodded. "I'm still translating the pages I found in the attic. Amable and Louis both eventually became doctors. Kylee and I thought it was important to include his information as an aside, because we don't know if we will find additional connections to the family through him."

"Well, I love it and can't wait to read all of the stories you have uncovered."

Joan set the book on the coffee table and her family gathered closer as she turned pages. Kirby tucked his hand in Sandi's arm and drew her to the side.

"Let's bundle up warm and go for a walk," he whispered. They slipped hand-in-hand from the room and got into coats.

"What's up?" Sandi asked as they stepped onto the front porch. White lights nestled in green garland case a warm glow.

"Wow. When Kyle mentioned Amable's name, I had cold chills—not negative ones, but just an odd sensation. Maybe a sense of *déjà vu*. I can't explain it."

"Maybe because you saw him during your travels?

"Hm, I don't know. But you remember that letter you gave me?"

"The one I kept forgetting to give you?" She had finally remembered the missive and delivered it to Kirby.

"Well, we have been rather preoccupied with ourselves." Kirby fingered her coat lapels, then brushed her lips with a tender kiss.

"True, we have." Sandi said when they broke from the embrace. Then she grabbed his lapels and planted one on him.

"Whew." Kyle shook his head. "Woman, you about made me forget why I wanted to come out here." He reached into his coat pocket.

"Ooh, ooh, another present?"

"Well, let's don't rush things." He pulled the yellowed envelope from his pocket. "I want you to read this."

"What is it?" Sandi removed a folded paper.

"Just read it."

Sandi angled her body for better light and began to read.

Dearest Kirby,

I wonder if this letter will ever reach you. It is not the miles that separate us but the years—many more years than the average person could imagine when they write a letter.

I stand here on the grounds of the newly-finished United States Naval Hospital in Portsmouth, where I will practice for a short time before I retire from the Navy. The same place where you will one day practice medicine.

When your mysterious travels brought you to the battlefields of Yorktown, you could not have known that the miracles of medicine you performed on the battlefield influenced both Louis and I to become doctors.

I remember standing outside the tent, just an orphan of ten, listening while you shared your incredible stories with Louis and Étienne. Although I was not a blood relation, Louis treated me as if I was a little brother and Étienne another son. I could not help but be amazed at how you looked so much like the two men to whom I owe a great deal. You were older than Louis and younger than Étienne, yet they were both your ancestral grandfathers!

Young boy that I was, I listened in awe as you talked about your life in the future and the marvels of your time. Carriages with wings that fly across the oceans carrying passengers, and boxes into which people could see and talk to each other. Had I ever told anyone of your fantastic journey, I would have been sent away to an insane asylum.

However, it was your actions during the last battles before the British surrendered that most influenced my future—in fact, you influenced nearly every aspect of the rest of my life.

You worked magic that no doctor of that time could have performed. I have to reemphasize that the moment I saw how you saved those soldiers, I planned to become a doctor and join the Navy. I did and eventually went to medical school and my journey began. I once sustained a leg injury in a fall on board ship, and was fortunate to recover, with only a limp to remind me. I remembered you had a slight limp. I imagine if we were ever to cross paths we would walk with a similar gait.

However, I never again saw the kind of battle that we fought at Yorktown, although during the war of 1812, I served at Craney Island. The encounter was short, and we suffered no casualties, but I ministered to several wounded. Étienne watched from the shores and lamented that he was not able to fight in this battle as he had fought for America as a young man!

When you saved Ian, son of the merchant Peter McDermott, you could not have known one thing. Ian would recover fully from his wounds and would go on to live a full life. He married and had children. His eldest child was a daughter, Iona, born in 1783.

Iona became my wife in 1803! We have one daughter, Aileen, married to sea captain Bruce McGowan, and their son is named Peter.

And here I stand today, together with Iona, gazing at this grand new hospital, and wonder what it will be like in your time, when

*you will one day work here. How many lives will be saved here, and
how many will be too wounded to save?*

*I listened intently as you told Louis and Étienne about the wars
America was fighting in your time, and the injury you sustained.
How I wished that I could have the amazing journey to your time as
you had to mine.*

*But alas, that shall not be, so I will finish my letter by saying
thank you for all you did, and for saving my future father in-law on
the battlefields of Yorktown. May the good Lord grace you all the
days of your life.*
Forever your servant,
Amable Fournier

Sandi stared ahead. "Kirby, what an amazing letter. I
remember that little boy during my time at the army
camp. He absolutely adored Louis and looked up to
Étienne. How honored I am to have shared some time
with him. Will you tell the others?"

"Not today, and only to the eight of us who know
what happened at the inn."

"Yes, I suppose that is wise."

"Hard to believe that a moment in time could have
such a profound result. He gives me too much credit.
Who's to say he and Louis would not have gone on to
become doctors anyway?"

"Possibly." Sandi took Kirby's hands and kissed them.
"But these hands—your hands—are healing hands. You
may patch broken limbs and bodies, but you do so much
more. You mend broken hearts." She pressed his hands
against her heart.

"Did you hear what Norrie told me when I got here
today?"

Sandi shook her head. "Between the kids shouting and
the dogs barking, I didn't hear anything."

"She said that Santa brought them presents here too, not just our house."

"Joan and Charles spoil her as if she is their own grandchild."

"Everyone becomes family around them, whether they are blood relations or not. But it's what Norrie said that got to me."

"What did she say?"

"She said 'our house.' Not her house, or Mama's house. She said, 'our house.'"

Sandi gasped. "Kirby, I'm so sorry."

"No, Sandi, don't be. Don't you know that is the best thing she could have said to me?" Kirby drew a long, slim box from his other pocket and handed it to her.

Sandi looked in his eyes, a tear glistening in the corners. She removed the ribbon and wrapping and lifted the lid of the velvet case to reveal a silver chain with a miniature version of the emerald in his ring.

"Oh, Kirby. I love this. It's beautiful." She drew the necklace from the box and held it to the light. Then she brushed her hair from her neck and handed the pendant to him. "Help me put it on?"

Kirby clasped the chain around her neck and fastened it, and then turned her to face him again. He started to speak, and she touched her fingertips to his lips.

"Do you think your parents would like to stay with the Dunbars—or come home with us tonight?"

Kirby's kiss was all the answer she needed.

EPILOGUE

Portsmouth, Virginia
1832

A warm breeze from the Elizabeth River drifted across the lawn where Dr. Amable Fournier strolled with his wife Iona. Streaks of gray hair at his temples showed more prominently in the bright sunlight, like strands of silver against black velvet. Iona swept back the lock of hair that always tumbled across her husband's forehead.

"The construction is nearly done," Amable said as his gaze swept over the building in front of him. There was a slight burr to his pronouncing of "nearly." He had long since lost the accent of his French-Canadian ancestry, but his speech often took on the tinge of a brogue that he had picked up from his more than forty years surrounded by his wife's Scottish family.

"I am glad that the workers rest on Sundays. On a beautiful day such as this, I can imagine the peace and quiet our injured military men will experience here in the future."

Iona sighed. "If only the war in eighteen-twelve could have been the last war our country faced, we would have no need of building a place to care for our wounded soldiers and sailors."

Amable shook his head, sorrow evident in his eyes. "Alas, we know that will not be the case. Kirby's strange visit revealed America was in a war during his lifetime, where he suffered leg injuries similar to mine—almost two hundred years from now."

"If I did not already know the story, I might think you were a madman to talk of a visitor from the future." She gave her husband's shoulder a teasing bump as the couple stopped at the foot of the stone steps leading to the new hospital.

"If there had been no visitor, you may never have been born, *mon amour*," he countered with a playful with his elbow. Then he placed his hand on the small of his wife's back to keep her from slipping as they ascended the sweeping stairs that had no banister.

They walked to the opening where the front doors would soon be in place. Amable pushed aside a heavy canvas covering the open portal so his wife could enter. He propped the flap open with several long boards he found nearby.

Their footsteps echoed as they crossed the main foyer of the impressive structure. Although nearly finished, signs of the workers' activity were still present. Sawhorses rested atop sheets of canvas that protected the marble floor where painters still needed to work on some areas. Amable barely glanced around the room or up to the vaulted ceiling. He had been inside during construction many times, first following the progress weekly, and then almost daily as the work neared completion.

"Soon you will be one of the first Naval physicians to practice in this new facility." Iona beamed with pride

"Only long enough to enjoy a few months of practice, *mon amour*," he reminded his wife. He patted his thigh. "It will soon be time to retire. I am afraid my injuries have caught up to me, and just to climb those stairs every day will cause even more pain to my leg." He turned to his right, down a long corridor of doors, and entered.

In mere days, the interior rooms would be painted. He had chosen the spot and had to act quickly. He walked the corridor, pausing by each door before continuing.

When he reached the room he had chosen, a slight

shiver—a gentle but not unpleasant sensation—coursed through him. He stepped over buckets of paint and a ladder in the center of the room and strode to a window overlooking the river. On either side of the framed glass, wood paneling covered the bottom half of the walls, the upper half unfinished gypsum. Amable took an envelope from the inside pocket of his waistcoat and slipped it between two studs framing the unfinished window. He tapped the paper down until it matched the edge of the wood in place on the lower half of the wall, so indiscernible that it should remain unnoticed by workers come Monday.

Iona observed her husband's action from the doorway. He had asked her to accompany him for this moment, but she would not intrude upon his time.

Finally, Amable seemed satisfied. He saluted and turned sharply on his heel. He nodded to his wife and without a word, offered her his arm.

"Do you really believe that my father would have died on the battlefield in Yorktown had not Kirby been there?" Iona asked as she slipped her hand in the crook of his arm.

Amable pondered, then shrugged. "I know not for sure what God intended for your papa, Iona. But no doctor of our time had the skills and knowledge Kirby possessed to perform such surgery. Even though I am not a blood relative to him, as neither were my dear friends Louis and Étienne, that one moment in time has influenced me like no other event in my life—save for our marriage," he added as Iona opened her mouth in protest. He winked and she smiled. "Your father would be proud to know he has a namesake in his great-grandson."

"I wish we had the magic power to travel in time as

Kirby did," Iona said.

"I think that is an occurrence reserved for a special few, for whom it can never be explained. It is a moment in time when everything that needs to be in place is present, perhaps it is the timing of the moon and stars that aligns with the presence of some inanimate object or magic portal that becomes the conduit of transportation."

"He came back in time. I wonder if others are able to travel into the future?"

"We will never know the answers, my sweet," Amable said as he drew her down the steps and turned to look out at the river.

"Then why did you bring the letter with you?"

Amable didn't answer. His eyes took on a faraway look, his gaze following a schooner sailing into the Portsmouth harbor. He waved, and thought he saw an answering movement. He jutted his chin toward the ship

"Our son-in-law sails into the harbor and our daughter and grandson wait anxiously for him. Shall we go to greet them?"

"Of course! But first, tell me why you brought the letter."

"Because, my dear, unlike our human bodies, inanimate things can stand the test of time. Years from now, someone will find that letter, and if it is the right moment in time, it will reach Kirby, to tell him in writing the words that I never had the chance to tell him in person. Although many people helped me throughout my life, I am a physician first and foremost because of Dr. Kirby Lawrence. And perhaps someday in the future, that letter will find its way into his hands, and he will know that he left a legacy even before he was born."

As the couple ambled toward the riverfront, they first strolled past Fort Nelson, and then their home overlooking the harbor. As they approached the docks, Amable shaded his eyes and smiled. "Peter is ready to greet his father."

A hundred yards away, his young grandson danced impatiently on the wharf as the ship slipped into its berth. Deckhands cast ropes to secure the lines as excited families pressed together to look for their loved ones. Shouts and whistles rose over the noise of the deckhands whenever someone spied their sailor.

"Stand still, Peter!" His mother's admonishment was not harsh, but her voice held the same note of excitement as his.

"Papa! Captain!" Jumping up and down, the young boy pumped his hands back and forth in a scissor-like fashion. His father scanned the crowd until his gaze landed on his son and wife, and he waved his arm in a wide arc.

"He sees us, he sees us, Mama."

"More likely, he heard you first, darling. But I am glad you are such a noisy little boy so that our captain can spot us right away."

At long last, the ship was secured, and an imposing man waited at the gangplank. Mother and son scrambled up to meet their seafaring captain.

The captain scooped his wife into an embrace that lifted her off her feet and kissed her. With a grimace and eye-roll, the boy saluted and said, "Permission to come aboard, Captain." The captain waved his son past without a break in the kiss he shared with his wife. He set her back on her feet, holding her close as they touched foreheads and shared a private moment until their son wiggled between them. The captain lifted his son and hugged him.

"So, my welcoming party is here to walk me home.

How did you time yourself to arrive as the same time as I did, Peter?"

"Mama and I were on the widow's walk and we could see your ship sailing down the river. We knew we had time to come down to meet you but we ran all the way anyway. I am happy to see you, Papa."

"And I am happy to see you." The captain threw back his head and laughed, then he locked eyes with his those of his wife. He gave her a saucy wink.

"When do you think I will be a captain and sail into Portsmouth Harbor, Papa?" the boy asked, using his finger to turn his father's chin so he could make eye contact.

"Oh, I predict—if you study hard and learn well—that you will bring a ship into Portsmouth Harbor in about the year of our Lord, eighteen fifty-five," Captain Angus McGowan teased.

Peter frowned. "How many years is that from now?"

Angus pondered, and said, "Twenty-eight. More than enough time for you to learn all there is to know about becoming the captain of your ship." The captain set his young son down and reached for his wife, waiting patiently with welcoming arms.

"I will sail the seven seas, Papa, every one of them. Maybe I will even sail to the edge of all time. Look, Mama, here comes Grandfather and Grandmother."

Amable and Iona waved as they sauntered up the gangplank to meet their daughter and son-in-law.

Peter scooted away from his parents and grandparents and pulled a small bottle from his pocket.

Inside was a scroll of heavy parchment paper, on which he had painstakingly written his name, the date and a short message. He told Mama what he wanted to say, which she wrote on her slate and then he copied her letters. Even though he couldn't spell all of the words properly, he knew his numbers and the alphabet. His mother helped him seal the cork stopper with wax to make a seaworthy container to protect his note.

He scrambled among sailors unloading cargo or greeting townsfolk who came to welcome the ship home. The boy reached the stern and stepped onto a wooden sea chest. He was just tall enough to fling the bottle into the river, as far as his little arm would allow.

On tiptoes, he peeked between the rails as the gentle waves caught his flagon, each swell taking it further from his sight.

A whirlpool caught the bottle. Peter's fascinated gaze followed the twirls until the dark amber vessel carrying his not disappeared from view.

Peter whispered the words he had written under the date of April 1832 and above his name.

"I will find you before you find me."

Find out more about Peter McGowan's time travels in
<u>The True Spirits Trilogy</u>
Coming in 2020

ABOUT THE AUTHOR

Author Allie Marie grew up in Virginia. Her favorite childhood pastime was reading Nancy Drew and Trixie Belden mysteries. When she embarked on a new vocation writing fiction after retiring from a career in law enforcement, it would have been understandable if her first book was a crime story. Researching her own family tree inspired her to write the True Colors Series instead. The other stories are patiently waiting their turn.

Her debut novel, *Teardrops of the Innocent: The White Diamond Story*, was a 2015 New England Readers' Choice Award Finalist in paranormal. The second in the series, *Heart of Courage: The Red Ruby Story* released in May 2016 and was voted Best Book in the 2017 IRC Readers' Choice Awards. February 2017 saw the release of the third book, *Voice of the Just: The Blue Sapphire Story*. The fourth book, *Hands of the Healer: The Christmas Emerald*, released in 2018 and won Best Cover in paranormal in the Rocky Mountain Cover Contest.

Child of Time: The Pearl Story is the fifth and final book in the True Colors Series. A spin-off of the series, The True Spirits Trilogy, is in the works.

Besides family, Allie's passions are travel and camping with her husband Jack.

Author photo courtesy of Laura Somers Photography

56107052R00121

Made in the USA
Columbia, SC
21 April 2019